FIN AND THE MEMORY CURSE

HELENKA STACHERA

Illustrated by Marco Guadalupi

PUFFIN

PUFFIN BOOKS

UK | USA | Canada | Ireland | Australia
India | New Zealand | South Africa

Puffin Books is part of the Penguin Random House group of companies
whose addresses can be found at global.penguinrandomhouse.com.

www.penguin.co.uk www.puffin.co.uk www.ladybird.co.uk

First published 2022

001

Typeset in 11.5/17pt Baskerville MT Std by Jouve (UK), Milton Keynes.
Printed and bound in Great Britain by Clays Ltd, Elcograf S.p.A.

The authorized representative in the EEA is Penguin Random House Ireland,
Morrison Chambers, 32 Nassau Street, Dublin D02 YH68

A CIP catalogue record for this book is available from the British Library

ISBN: 978-0-241-49133-1

All correspondence to:
Puffin Books, Penguin Random House Children's
One Embassy Gardens, 8 Viaduct Gardens, London SW11 7BW

For Kat

Hackney Marsh, London, 1866

'Oy! Snot's got more than me!'

Fin rolled her eyes. 'Shut up, George. No he don't.'

The three of them, Fin, Snot and George, were huddled in front of the cold fireplace, eating a breakfast of stale bread dipped in the fat from last night's sausages.

Fin was in charge of making sure the portions were equal. 'I'm trying my best to share it out fair,' she said. 'Be easier if I could see what I was doing.'

It was six o'clock in the morning and rosy dawn light was stealing through the streets of London. But Ma's attic, what with it having no windows, was as dark and dismal as an undertaker's.

Fin and Snot were squashed up together in the sagging armchair, while George had bravely plonked himself in Ma's rocker, despite the hiding he'd get if he was caught. He kept a sharp ear out and flinched at every noise that floated up from the alley below.

Small sat at Fin's feet, tongue hanging out, polishing a patch on the sooty floor with his tail.

'Don't worry,' Fin said to him. 'I ain't forgotten about you.' She wiped the end of the loaf round the pan, scraping up all the tastiest burnt bits and threw it to him. The little Jack Russell terrier snatched it from the air and snaffled it down in one gulp.

Just then, there came the thud of a heavy footstep at the bottom of the makeshift steps leading to the door of the attic. The whole building trembled and the three foundlings sat up, eyes wide.

'That'll be Ma!' George leaped from the rocker and shot behind the armchair, trying not to look guilty. There were several more footsteps, a short silence during which Fin imagined Ma leaning on the brickwork and catching her breath, then the thudding continued and, finally, the door flew open and hung at an angle on its single hinge.

Ma Stump filled the doorway, blocking out the morning light. She was six feet tall and much the same around. If asked, she put her extraordinary size down to

an excess of meat pies as a young 'un, her uncle having been a butcher.

Out of habit, she ducked her head as she came in, to avoid banging it on the rafters. 'Mornin', foundlings,' she said, a big smile on her face.

Fin let out a breath; Ma was in a good mood.

'Where've you been?' Snot asked.

Ma made them wait for her reply. She dusted herself down, lowered herself into her chair and set it rocking, back and forth. 'Met a man down the Tripe and Eel.'

The foundlings exchanged a fearful glance. Ma's last gentleman friend, who she had declared 'a real charmer', had turned out to be a bludger, and Snot still had the wonky nose to prove it. In the end, he'd made off with most of the furniture and, most upsettingly for Ma, a large bottle of Navy rum she had put aside for Christmas.

Ma burst out laughing when she saw their faces. 'Not *that* kind of a man! It weren't romance, it were a business meeting.'

'Well,' Fin said, 'we was worried. Me and Small went out looking last night when you didn't come back.'

'*Awww*, now that's why you're my favourite.' Ma gave Fin a playful pinch, leaving an angry mark on her cheek.

'What was this business meeting about then?' George asked.

Ma folded her arms and nodded in satisfaction. 'I got a new customer, and a quality one at that.' She stopped rocking and leaned forward. 'I'd go as far as to say he's a customer of the very best sort.'

Fin smiled. 'More money than sense?'

'That's right, my girl!' Ma rubbed her meaty hands together. 'A Mr Canary, an apothecary from over in Holloway. He's willing to cough up ten shillings for a dozen slimy bloodsuckers.'

George whistled. 'Ten shillings!' he said. 'Could buy a lot of sausages for that.'

Snot swiped excitedly at his nose, adding another shining trail to the collection covering his sleeve. 'That's more than double the usual price.'

'What was he like, this Mr Canary?' George asked.

Snot sniffed. 'Must've been a right toff, eh?'

Ma chuckled. 'Oh, he was full of the airs and graces all right, but no – more like one of them what's *trying* to be a toff. But I don't judge. His money's as good as anyone's.'

'Well, he can have as many of 'em as he likes,' Fin said. 'We got plenty back there.' She jerked her head towards the stack of bottles and tins piled in the corner. Each had airholes punched in the top, and contained grass and reed stalks and a number of leeches she had caught during the summer. Fin was a skilful leecher. She'd even grown her thumbnails especially long for digging under the slimy creatures' heads and levering them off. Trouble was, bleeding wasn't the popular cure it used to be, and Ma hadn't managed to sell any leeches for months.

'No,' Ma said. 'Them's no good. He wants 'em *fresh*.' She nodded towards Fin. 'You'll have to go out and fetch some more.'

'Why me?'

'Cos yer only eleven,' Ma said. 'And that makes you the youngest.'

'Yeah,' George said with a smirk. 'And the ugliest!'

Fin rolled her eyes. It was always the same. There were only downsides to being the youngest.

'But it's November,' she said. 'How am I supposed to catch a dozen this time of year?'

Ma shrugged. 'Better get on with it then, and mind you do. We can't afford to turn our noses up at ten shillings.'

Snot sniffed noisily. 'It ain't fair, just cos Fin's the youngest.'

Everyone went quiet.

Ma blinked a couple of times and slowly swivelled her head towards Snot. 'You know, I could *swear* I heard somebody say something . . .'

Snot drew in another noisy bubbling breath, ready to say more, but Fin caught his eye and shook her head. She gave him a smile too, to let him know she appreciated it, but what was the point? Snot would get a walloping and Fin would still have to go.

She got to her feet. 'Come on then, Small. Let's fetch Dolly and get on with it.'

'No, not Dolly. No donkeys,' Ma said. 'You'll have to go in yerself. He wants 'em human-caught.'

Fin was baffled. 'What for? They's just the same peeled off a donkey's leg as my own.'

'P'raps he's a vampire.' Ma winked. 'Anyways, who cares?' She rubbed the tips of her fingers and thumb together. 'The price he's paying, I'd get the bloomin' Queen to catch 'em for him.'

Fin fetched her leeching stick and an empty collecting tin from the mantelpiece and headed for the door with Small at her heels. Before she left, she grabbed the tattered boots that were in the corner. 'I'm taking these,' she said, and she narrowed her eyes at Snot and George, daring them to say no. George looked as if he might, but Snot put a hand on his arm.

'Fair enough, its cold out on the marsh,' Snot said.

There was only one pair of boots between the three of them. They fitted Snot well and were getting too small for George. Fin stuffed them with straw, partly to plug the holes, but also because they were still far too big for her.

She was halfway through the door when Ma called out from her rocker, 'Fin? I know you'll do yer best. You're a good girl. Practically me own flesh an' blood.'

Fin couldn't help smiling back at her. It wasn't everyday she got that kind of praise. Ma could be harsh, but she told a good story and laughed a lot, and when Fin was in her good books, she could feel the warmth of it.

She slammed the door behind her and climbed down the staircase to the street, stopping on the bottom step, as she often did.

This was where Ma Stump had found her, abandoned, more than ten years ago.

When Fin was small, she'd asked when her mother would be coming to fetch her. 'Ooh now, let me see . . .' Ma had said, scratching her head and counting the time out on her fingers. 'That would be . . . around about . . . *never*!'

Snot and George had laughed themselves hoarse at that. They were unwanted foundlings themselves, but being a few years older than Fin, had grown hardened to the fact.

'What do you lot know?' Fin had said. 'She might.'

Ma shook her head. 'Who leaves a baby wrapped in yesterday's newspaper like a bag o' chips, and means to come back for it?'

It was a convincing argument, but Fin didn't stop hoping. She longed for a mum and dad, a family of her own. Perhaps she'd been lost or mislaid, and one day they'd realize and come back for her. It *could* happen, couldn't it?

Like any foundling, she was prone to daydreaming about how she'd ended up on Ma Stump's doorstep. She had no idea *why* she'd been abandoned, but she remembered it happening.

Ma said she was being stupid. 'You was a baby. No one remembers that.'

But Fin was sure she could. It wasn't the usual kind of memory. No. She'd been too young for that. It was more like a *feeling*. A feeling of being held in her mother's warm, safe arms. But there was one thing she remembered as clear as the Bow Bells on a still morning: her mother's face, looking down at her, full of longing and sadness.

After that, the cold crept in.

It was Fin's most precious memory, and whenever she was unhappy she would remember that feeling of being loved and hold it close. In a world that deemed her valueless, it made her feel she was worth something.

She glanced back up at the attic. It was at the top of an old tenement that leaned precariously over the Lea, the river that wound its way through this part of

Hackney. For decades, the building had been hungrily absorbing the damp humours that rose from the water into its crumbling bricks and mortar. Ma said the house was more liquid than solid and predicted it would soon slide down the muddy banks and topple into the river. The building had once been grand, but when fashionable London moved west it had been abandoned and left for the poor to inhabit, but not before everything of value had been stripped out: the marble and slate from the fireplaces, the brass handles and hinges, the glass in the windows. Even the staircases had been sold for firewood, and now the only way to the upper floor was via the set of makeshift steps propped against the outside of the building. Ma's attic wasn't pretty and it wasn't comfortable, but Fin was grateful for the only home she had known.

She sighed. 'Come on, Small. We got work to do, and at least it ain't raining.'

Small trotted ahead, tail up and nose to the ground, following the familiar raised path that wound between the ponds. In the summer, the marshes were busy with reed-cutters. All the leechers from thereabouts would've been out, either wading into the ponds themselves, or if they could get one, sending in a donkey or a goat. But at this time of year, the marshes were deserted, and all the better for it, Fin thought. After being squashed up with three others in Ma's dank attic, she prized the huge skies and open spaces of the wild and beautiful marsh. Out here, a body could escape the press of other people, the smogs and smells of the overcrowded city. Out here, Fin could really breathe.

She had first learned to love the marshes during the time of the Great Stink, eight years ago now, when the Thames had overflowed with raw sewage and the bloated animal corpses from the abattoirs. How could anyone forget that baking hot summer, the dreadful fog that drifted off the Thames and choked London half to death?

The odd thing was, although Snot and George were a couple of years older than Fin, neither of them remembered anything about the Great Stink at all. 'We was too young,' they said.

But Fin's memory was like a priceless diamond, flashing with colour and clarity. It wasn't only important things she remembered, it was *everything*. If asked, she could have listed the names and scores of the leading England wicket-takers back in 1860 (the winner being John 'Foghorn' Jackson with 109 wickets). She wasn't even interested in cricket, but George was, and that year he didn't stop going on about it. Fin had only been five years old, but once told, she never forgot. Sometimes

Fin wished she didn't have her unerring ability to remember things. After all, there were some scenes best covered over and forgotten. But however useless or painful a memory, it was stuck in her head, whether she liked it or not.

There was no breeze that day. The quiet waters stretched out before Fin and Small, still shrouded in a blur of early-morning mist. Fin stopped at a shallow pond, hitched up her skirts and got in. The water was so icy it made her gasp and, for a moment, she stood still, gritting her teeth against the cold. She waded to a clump of yellowing reeds on the other side of the pond and poked her leeching stick about at the roots to encourage the creatures from their hiding places. Then there was nothing to do but wait.

It was a nasty job, standing around all day in freezing water, waiting for a bite. But by late afternoon, Fin had managed to catch a dozen of the slimy worms.

'Done it!' Fin hauled herself out on to the bank and flopped down next to Small.

He whined and laid his head in her lap.

'It ain't as bad as it looks,' she said, stroking his soft ears.

Fin lay back and gazed up at the sky. It was her favourite time of day on the marshes. The sun was low, shading the bellies of the clouds rose gold. Great flocks of starlings massed and swirled above the meandering loops of the misty river, before dropping as one to roost among the reeds. The sun slipped below the horizon, and as the light began to fade from the sky, a gibbous moon showed her silvery face.

The mists were rising and evening was coming on, but Fin wasn't worried. She knew the marshes like the back of her hand and could've made it home with her eyes shut. Anyways, Small would sniff out the pathways and it was easy to follow his little white body, which shone in the gloom, even on the darkest night.

3

Someone called her name and Fin turned to see Snot marching across the marshes towards her.

'Got the leeches?'

Fin nodded. 'What about you? How was work?'

'It were a tough day.' He held out his hands, which were red-raw and peeling from the lime they used at the laundry. Even so, Fin would have swapped jobs any day; laundry work was warm and it didn't cost any blood. Snot was a couple of years older than Fin, but he was just as thin and no taller either. He used to be a chimney sweep, but although he was the perfect size, the soot ruined his lungs and worsened the catarrh problem that had earned him his name.

He sat down next to Fin and pulled an apple out of his pocket. He held it up to the light, then polished it on his trousers before taking a big bite.

'Where'd you get that?' Fin asked.

'Where d'you think?'

'What? You managed to get over that massive wall?'

'Might've done.' Snot took another bite and the juice ran down his chin. The apple was burnished red and shiny. It looked delicious. It *smelled* even better.

Fin tried not to stare as Snot took his next bite. '*Mmm*,' he said, 'this might just be the best apple *ever*.'

Small whined and Fin turned away, close to tears.

'Shut up, Snot! If you ain't gonna share, go and eat your bloomin' scrumped apple somewhere else!'

Snot raised one eyebrow. 'Hang on . . . What's this I just found in my pocket?' He pulled out another apple and threw it to her.

Fin was almost too cross to thank him. He teased her just as much as George did, but unlike George, Snot had a heart of gold underneath. He always looked out for her, and stood in the way when George's taunts threatened to grow fists.

When Small had munched up the apple cores, the three of them made their way back to town. They crossed the bridge and, as they often did, headed along the high street and stopped to look in the window of the toy shop. It was almost dark now. The shopkeeper had lit the gas lamps so that the window shone with light and colour.

'Look at them!' Snot pointed to the red-and-white candy sticks, the bags of striped humbugs, the boxes of marzipan and fudge. But Fin wasn't so interested in sweets, or the hoops and the jack-in-a-box, nor in the porcelain dolls in their silk dresses and their real-hair golden ringlets.

Instead, her eye was drawn to a stack of books set right in the middle of the display. There was a picture on the cover of a girl with playing cards flying all around her. She had her arms thrown up, as if the cards were attacking her and she was trying to fend them off.

Fin pressed her nose against the glass. One of the copies had been opened, and propped up facing outwards. If Fin screwed her eyes up, she could just make it out, and she read some of it out loud to Snot.

'What?' Snot said. 'A talking rabbit in a waistcoat? With a pocket watch?' He shook his head. 'And then this girl falls down a rabbit hole? Not very likely!'

Fin gave him a shove. 'It's a *story*. You got to use your imagination.'

Snot pressed his forehead to the glass and peered at the book. 'How d'you manage to make sense of all them black squiggles?'

'You know how,' Fin said. 'George showed both of us.'

'Did he?' Snot screwed his face up, trying to remember. 'When was that?'

'After he got orphaned by the cholera and came to live with us, remember? He was showing off how clever he was cos he'd been to that ragged school.'

Shortly after his arrival at Ma Stump's attic, George had taught both Fin and Snot the letters and the sound each one made. Snot never got the hang of it, and George himself soon forgot through lack of practice. But Fin's diamond-bright memory made learning easy. She read everything she saw – the names on streets and shops, the advertising posters plastered on the outside of buildings, the greasy out-of-date newspapers their chips came wrapped in. Once she'd seen a word and worked it out, she never forgot it again.

Of course, she'd never so much as touched an actual book, and she gazed longingly at the ones in the shop window. Wouldn't it be wonderful to escape her own dreary life and go on an adventure? Or even better, what would it be like to be an author, someone who made a living making things up and writing them down? She imagined herself in a few years, sitting at a desk, dipping a pen in a pot of purple ink. Given the chance, she'd make up stories and lives that were better and happier than her own. There would be endless breakfasts and dinners and even banquets, and no one would ever go to bed hungry.

She pushed the thought away. For a start, she couldn't write, and everyone knew books were written by posh people anyway. No, the best she could hope for was to be apprenticed to Sally Gamble in a year or two, like Snot was, and make a living doing rich people's laundry.

Just then, a family approached. A mum and dad, a girl about Fin's age and a little boy. They stood together, talking about the sweets and toys in the window. Then the father scooped the little boy up in his arms and they all went inside the shop.

Fin watched all this out of the corner of her eye, and when she turned to Snot she saw that he was watching too. A thin smile came to Snot's face as the little boy pointed to the window, and the shop assistant leaned in and took down a bag of sweets. Fin didn't have to ask what the thin smile meant; Snot was a foundling, like her.

'We don't need them,' Snot said. 'What did they ever do for us 'cept abandon us? Anyways, we got Ma.'

Out of habit, Fin nodded her agreement. And Snot was right, they'd got lucky with Ma. Still, Fin kept hold of that memory of her mother's face. She no longer mentioned it out loud, knowing she'd be ridiculed. She kept it to herself, buried in her heart.

'Come on,' she said, turning away from the bright window. 'We'd better be getting back. It's nearly dinner time.'

When Fin, Snot and Small got back, Ma Stump was hunched over the fire, tongs in hand, frying sausages in a pan. 'Got 'em?' she said, straightening up.

Fin lifted the lid on the collecting tin and showed her the contents. Ma counted the dozen under her breath and nodded, satisfied.

George was lounging in the armchair and held out his hand, 'Let's be 'avin' a look.'

'Move over then,' Fin said, elbowing her way on to the armrest before passing him the tin.

George lifted the lid and peered inside cautiously. 'Ooh, there's some right fat ones there. You done well today, girl.'

'Too right! And it's hungry work,' Fin said, reaching out to grab a sausage.

'Get off!' Ma rapped the back of her hand with the tongs. 'They ain't ready, and anyway, there's no dinner for you until you deliver them leeches.'

'Can't it wait till morning?' Fin said, eyeing the pan.

'No, it can't. Canary wants 'em fresh, remember?'

Fin huffed in annoyance, but it was no use arguing with Ma where business was concerned.

'And mind he pays in full,' Ma said. 'Ten shillings. As agreed.' The pan was spitting fat and she rolled her sleeves up, revealing forearms like a pair of scalded hams. 'Don't worry, I'll save you a nice juicy sausage.'

Fin narrowed her eyes at George. 'And make sure that greedy gib-face don't steal my supper, like last time.'

'Whatever can she mean?' George said, all innocence. 'I never ate your sausage. It jumped out the pan and escaped down a crack between the floorboards.'

Both Snot and George rolled around laughing at that.

'That's enough now, you two,' Ma chided. She turned back to Fin and gave her an affectionate cuff round the ear. 'Off you go then.'

4

Fin clamped a hand over her nose and headed out with Small at her heels. Ma often said the noxious aromas that came off the river were so thick, you could 'practically chew 'em'. But that evening, the smell of rubbish and sewage and fish heads that rose from the sluggish waters were somewhat masked by the gut-wrenching whiff of glue from the knacker's yard next door and the sickening stink of whale oil wafting from the hemp factory across the road.

The dark alley on which Ma's attic was situated was a well-known place for muggings, but Fin wasn't worried – Small might be, well, *small*, but he was more than a match for any scrawny thief. In any case, as Fin reached the high street she bumped into Sergeant

Malone on his rounds. Small jumped up, planting his muddy paws on the policeman's spotless trousers, but he only laughed and bent down to give Small a pat on the head.

He glanced at Fin. 'Where you off to, then? Up to no good, I suppose?'

Fin showed him the collecting tin. 'I'm off to swindle an apothecary.'

'Leeching? At this time of year?'

'Tell me about it!' Fin said, thinking ruefully of the sausages back at Ma's.

Sergeant Malone straightened up and peered into Fin's face. 'Must've been cold out on the marshes. You look like you could do with a decent dinner.'

It wasn't the first time the sergeant had taken pity on Fin and offered to buy her a pie or a bag of chips. In Fin's experience, most coppers were out for a backhander, but Sergeant Malone was different. He was one of the few people Small had never bitten, and Small was never wrong about who to trust. People might smile and talk the talk, but they couldn't get past Small's nose – he could sniff a rogue out at fifty paces.

'Thanks,' Fin said. 'But I'm all right – Ma's doing us sausages. Only I have to deliver these bloomin' worms first.'

'Right you are,' he said. 'But the missus is baking this week, and she says you and Snot are to come round for tea.'

Fin agreed enthusiastically, since Mrs Malone was known for her excellent cakes. She waved goodbye, then she and Small went across the square to the Tripe and Eel, where Ma had said the apothecary was staying.

Away from the factories and the river, Fin drew in a deep lungful of air. The fragrant smell of kidney pudding wafted from the open window of the pub kitchen. The apple Snot had given her was the only thing Fin had eaten since breakfast and her stomach rumbled.

'Smell that?' she said to Small. 'Ain't fair, is it? The others are all warm and snug back at Ma's and tucking into their dinner, while we're out in the cold with a tin of leeches.'

Small whined and pressed himself against her leg. He always understood. There were a few good 'uns, like Sergeant Malone, Fin thought, but if she had to choose between dogs and humans, dogs were by far the better choice.

She was about to go in when the door to the saloon bar burst open and a red-faced drunk stumbled out, leaning heavily on the arm of a street urchin. Fin dodged out of the way as the man threw up on the cobbles.

'Tha's it,' the urchin said soothingly. He gave Fin a wink and stealthily removed a purse from the drunk's pocket. 'Better out than in.'

Fin stepped round them and went inside. The taproom was packed. There was laughing and screeching and singing and dancing and Fin thought she'd never fight her way through the sea of swaying bodies, but Small growled and nipped at ankles until he'd cleared a path for her to the bar.

'Evenin', what can I do you for?' the landlord said, shouting to be heard above the din.

'I'm looking for Mr Canary.' Fin held up the collecting tin. 'I've got his leeches for him.'

'He's expecting you.' The landlord spat on a shot glass, polished it with a filthy rag and placed it next to the others on the shelf. 'He's out back, having a bit of dinner.'

Fin had never been in the private dining room at the Tripe and Eel, but she'd caught a glimpse once or twice when the door was open. It was kept nice for the better class of guests, the sort who didn't like to mingle with the riff-raff in the public bar. Just the place, Fin thought, for the type of toffee-nosed customer who insisted on fresh, *human*-caught leeches.

The landlord let her behind the bar and showed her through. There was no spit and sawdust here. A fire blazed in the grate and, although they'd seen better days, there were tasselled drapes at the windows and a Turkey rug on the floorboards.

Mr Canary was the only person there. As soon as Small caught his scent, he started growling and let out one sharp bark, which meant the apothecary would prove to be worse than the usual petty thieves and cads they came across.

Fin quietened him. 'All right, Small,' she whispered. 'He's a bad 'un, but he's a paying customer, and Ma said we got to be nice.'

Mr Canary waved Fin over to his table, in the middle of which sat a huge and succulent-looking game pie. Fin's mouth started watering.

She put the collecting tin on the table. ''Ere's yer worms. Ten shillings, as was agreed.'

The apothecary opened the tin and, sticking his nose inside, closed his eyes and took a deep breath, as if smelling a bunch of the finest roses. 'Human-caught?'

Fin nodded.

He pawed excitedly at the silk cravat he wore. It might once have been a jaunty sunshine yellow, but now it carried the stains of many gravy dinners, and the London smog had long ago cured it to the colour of a smoked haddock. 'You can guarantee it?'

'Oh yes,' Fin said. 'Since they was collected by yours truly.'

Mr Canary turned his round, black eyes on Fin. He had a sharp nose and narrow face, not unlike the ferret Ma used to keep for the rats.

'In which case the wounds will still be bleeding?' He grinned, his thin lips peeling from teeth almost the colour of his yellow cravat, and Fin cringed in disgust.

Just then, there was a rap at the door.

'A lady to see you, Mr Canary,' the landlord's wife said, and she stood aside to allow a smartly dressed woman to come into the dining room.

The apothecary shoved Fin out of the way and got to his feet. 'Do I have the priviledge of addressing the honourable Lady Worth?'

The lady nodded once. 'Indeed.' She cast a look around her, seemingly unimpressed by the luxury of the decorations. For a moment her keen blue eyes rested on Fin, but seeing nothing of interest there, moved on. Her black bonnet and dress weren't fancy, but Fin could tell from the cut and sheen of the spotless fabric that they had cost a pretty penny, not to mention her button-backed gloves trimmed with fur. Lady Worth looked aloof and more than a little formidable, as if life's dirt and filth would never dare attach itself to *her* person.

Small trotted over and sniffed at the hem of her dress and, for the first time, the lady smiled. 'Oh, what a handsome Jack Russell!' She leaned down and gave

Small a pat. Fin was about to warn her to be careful, but to her surprise Small didn't nip her, but only wagged his tail instead. 'My favourite breed,' she said. 'Where did you get him?'

''E was with me when I was found.'

'Found?'

Fin nodded. 'Yes, found, ma'am. On Ma Stump's doorstep. Wrapped in newspapers, I was, and only a babber. Small was right there next to me, protecting me, Ma says.'

Mr Canary stepped in front of Fin. 'Stop bothering the lady with your blathering,' he hissed. He turned back to Lady Worth and motioned for her to sit. 'May I offer you some refreshment?'

Lady Worth gave the game pie a haughty look. 'I think not.' But she deigned to perch on the edge of the chair the apothecary offered.

'Well, this is a little awkward,' Mr Canary said, folding and refolding the napkin in his lap. 'You see, I was expecting Doctor Hunt. I take it you've come for the . . . um . . .' He hesitated, perhaps wondering what name for the slimy clingers was appropriate in the presence of a lady.

'The leeches?' Lady Worth prompted. 'Yes. Unfortunately, Doctor Hunt is indisposed and I could not wait.'

Mr Canary nodded. 'I was devastated to hear of your daughter's illness.'

Lady Worth flinched. 'I *beg* your pardon?'

'Oh! How impertinent of me!' Mr Canary feverishly screwed his napkin into a ball. 'I did not mean to assume –'

Lady Worth held up a hand and cut him short. 'The leeches, if you please, Mr Canary.'

The apothecary's eyes darted from Lady Worth to Fin to the collecting tin that still sat on the table. Fin smiled as she realized his problem – he didn't want Lady Worth to see him pay Fin ten shillings for the leeches when he was about to charge *her* two guineas.

He tried to wave Fin away. 'Tell your mistress I'll settle up with her tomorrow.'

But Fin stood her ground and Small growled and bared his teeth. 'Oh no you don't, mister. I'll get no supper and a good hiding if I go back empty-handed.'

The apothecary looked furious, but he could hardly take her to task in front of Lady Worth. He patted his pockets and reluctantly brought out his purse.

Fin held out her hand. 'That'll be ten shillings.'

Lady Worth gasped and Fin was about to agree that it was indeed an outrageous sum, when she saw the lady was staring at her outstretched fingers.

Fin was not altogether surprised by her reaction because, on Fin's right hand she had six fingers rather than five. The extra digit sat right next to her little finger and was a bit smaller. She'd had to put up with a lot of teasing about it from Snot and George, and occasionally Ma, and the street urchins thereabouts always asked for a gander. Fin never took it to heart. As far as she was concerned, it was just one of those things, and no different to her long hair being red, or George having big feet. Posh people hardly ever noticed. Only, this lady was now staring goggle-eyed and had gone as pale as a bedsheet.

'What you starin' at?' Fin thrust her hand under Lady Worth's nose. 'It ain't my fault.'

'No, of course not.' Lady Worth fanned her face with a hand, and after a moment seemed to recover herself. 'I'm so sorry, you must think me very rude.'

Fin shrugged. 'Can't say I'm not used to it.'

'I'd like to make amends,' the lady said. 'You mentioned you hadn't had any dinner yet, so would you like something to eat?'

'What, me? In 'ere? With you and 'im?'

Lady Worth nodded. 'The pie looks just about edible.' Without a word to Mr Canary, she cut a thick slice and put it on a plate, where it sat, steaming invitingly. 'I imagine your dog – Small, wasn't it? – might be hungry too,' and she dug some of the meaty innards out of the pie with a spoon, put them in a bowl and set it down on the floor. Then she patted the chair next to her. 'Come and sit here with me.'

Fin couldn't help being suspicious. Mr Canary looked like he'd been struck by lightning and the lady was being . . . well, she was being *too* nice. But the pie did smell delicious. Small was wolfing down his portion, and Mr Canary had already eaten some, which meant it couldn't be poisoned . . .

She sat down, picked up the pie and took a huge bite.

As Fin ate, the lady bombarded her with questions about who she lived with and where. 'And what is your age?' she asked.

'Eleven,' Fin answered between mouthfuls. 'Far as I know.' Fin couldn't understand why she was so interested, since she could tell by the way the lady looked at her, the way she held a perfumed handkerchief to her nose, that she found her distasteful. And the look on the lady's face when Fin dropped her aitches! Nonetheless, Lady Worth kept on asking and, strangely, Mr Canary seemed just as interested in what Fin had to say. It was all rather odd.

'And your name?' Lady Worth continued.

'Fin.'

'Unusual. I haven't heard that one before.'

'It's short for Fingers,' Fin said.

Lady Worth looked horrified. 'That's not a name . . . it's an insult!'

'Not where I come from, it ain't.' Fin explained that there was no harm in it. Apart from George, everyone who lived in Ma's attic was named according to their peculiarities. There was Small, of course, and Ma Stump herself, who had acquired her moniker from her heavy way of walking. Fin would have gone on to spell out the reason behind Snot's name, but she decided against it, seeing as how they were eating.

Even so, it can't have been a pretty sight, Fin trying to answer the lady's endless questions, while at the same time gulping down as much pie as she could.

Finally, Lady Worth asked, 'Do you have any idea who your parents were, or what happened to them?'

Pie or no pie, Fin was tired of all these personal questions. 'Like I already mentioned,' she said pointedly, 'I were only little.'

At this, Lady Worth seemed to have learned all she wanted to know. While Fin continued to eat, the lady sat in silence, biting her lip and staring off into the distance. Meanwhile, Mr Canary eyed Fin, like a prize goose he was fattening for Christmas.

At last, Fin could eat no more. 'I'm stuffed,' she said, pushing her plate away. Lady Worth jumped, as if she was surprised Fin was still there. She gave her a tight smile.

'Excellent . . .' For a moment, she seemed flustered. She glanced at Fin and opened her mouth again, as if to say something else, but then she shuddered, shook her head, and shut it again.

Suddenly, she pushed her chair away from the table. 'I must take my leave of you,' she announced, and she reached for the collecting tin on the table and stood up. 'Mr Canary, you may send your bill to the house.' Without so much as a look or a word to Fin, she turned on her heel. 'I bid you a good evening.'

When she had gone, the apothecary turned his yellow smile on Fin. 'You know, I'm looking for an apprentice to help out in my shop in Holloway. A bright girl like you –'

Small bared his teeth and growled at the idea and Fin shook her head. 'Ma would never let me go. I bring in a good wage, see, an' I'm like a daughter to her, Ma says . . . Anyways, thanks for the grub.'

Fin and Small left the dining room and pushed into the noise and carousing of the public bar. They weaved round the beer drunks, who were still standing, and the gin drunks, who were not, and stepped out into the quiet street. Fog off the marshes had invaded the town and the haloed street lamps seemed to float, like stemless blooms in the darkness. They hurried across the bridge, along River Alley and up the steps to Ma Stump's attic.

Inside, the fire was blazing. It was wonderfully warm and Ma, Snot and George were all sparked out. Fin peered into the frying pan. Just as well she and Small had been given a bit of that pie, since there was not a single sausage left between them.

Fin was about to settle down herself when there came a loud knocking, and Small rushed to the door, barking and growling. When Fin opened up she found the apothecary on the doorstep.

'Oh, Mr Canary! We wasn't expecting you.'

He gave her a ratty smile. 'I'd like a word with Ma Stump, if you please.'

Fin narrowed her eyes. She was sure the man was up to something, but he paid well, and as Ma always said, money talks louder than good. 'You'd better come in, then,' she said.

'Customer!' she announced, giving Ma a poke.

'Who is it this time of night?' Ma sat up and rubbed her eyes. 'And make that bleedin' dog shut up an' all!'

'It's Mr Canary,' Fin said. 'Seems a dozen bloodsuckers ain't enough for him.'

Ma mopped her brow and got up to greet the visitor. She banished Snot and George from the armchair and settled Mr Canary into its ancient greasy embrace. 'Will you take a tot of rum?' she asked him.

'I'd be delighted, madam,' Mr Canary said. Then he caught sight of the murky bottle Ma proffered and he rubbed his knee and winced theatrically. 'Er . . . if only my gout would allow it.'

'So,' Ma said, collapsing back into her rocking chair. 'How might I be of service, Mr Canary? I'd be happy to oblige with a regular supply of leeches. Just say the word.'

'It's not the leeches I'm here for . . .' Mr Canary cleared his throat. 'I've come about the girl.'

Fin retreated behind Ma's rocking chair. 'I already told him, I'm not interested in working in no shop.' She put her hand on Ma's shoulder. 'Ain't that right, Ma?'

Ma Stump reached up and patted Fin's hand. 'You leave it to me, love.' She turned back to Mr Canary. 'The girl, you say?'

'I'm looking for an apprentice, and the girl here . . . well, she's a little rough around the edges but she seems bright enough.'

'Cheek of it!' Fin huffed. 'Tell him no, Ma.'

Ma waved Fin away. 'Thing is, Mr Canary, why would I want to apprentice her? She's a good girl, knows when to keep her mouth shut, and she don't smell too bad.'

'See?' Fin said. 'Didn't I tell you?'

After being hoiked out of the armchair, Snot and George had fallen straight back to sleep, but now Snot got up and came and stood next to Fin. 'What's going on?' he whispered.

'Nothing to worry about,' Fin replied. 'Ma's got it covered. She'll be sending him packing in a minute.'

Only Ma didn't send him packing. 'Why, the girl's like a daughter to me,' she said, pressing her huge fist to her heart. 'But what's more pertinent,' she continued, 'Fingers here brings in a wage.' She smiled sweetly at Mr Canary. '*More* than pays for her keep, if you see what I mean?'

Mr Canary smiled back. 'Madam, you are making yourself abundantly clear. What say I offer you . . . ten pounds?'

Ma burst out laughing.

Fin joined in. 'Who does he think 'e is? Ten pound? You can't *buy* me.' She gave Snot a nudge, expecting him to join in with the joke too, but he just stared at Ma with a frown on his face.

'What's going on, Ma?' he said.

Ma seemed not to have heard. 'You know what? I've got a sudden yearning for a bottle o' stout. Snot,

38

why don't you run down the Tripe an' Eel and fetch it for me?'

Snot clenched his fists. 'But –'

'Now off you go,' Ma said menacingly. 'And you won't bother hurrying back, if you know what's good for you.'

Snot looked at Fin, but she gave him a nod to let him know he shouldn't argue. She was as good as family, and Ma was only winding the apothecary up.

When Snot had gone Ma turned back to Mr Canary. 'Now, where was we?'

'I'd just offered ten pounds for the girl,' the apothecary said.

Fin huffed. 'Didn't you 'ear what Ma just said? I'm practically like a daughter –'

'Call it fifteen then.' Mr Canary pulled his wallet out of his pocket with a flourish and laid it on the armrest.

'Well now,' Ma said. She took out a grubby handkerchief and started fanning herself. 'Here's a turn of events.'

'Tell him you ain't selling, Ma!' Fin said.

Ma hushed her. 'Let's just hear what the gentleman has to say, shall we?' She put a foot on the grate and pushed off, setting her chair rocking.

'Five and twenty pounds!' Mr Canary announced.

There was a sharp intake of breath and Ma's rocking chair went into a gallop.

It was an awful lot of money, but Fin knew Ma would never sell her to an old rogue like Mr Canary. 'Why can't you understand?' she said to the apothecary. 'It's not about the money. We're like family. Tell him, Ma.'

Ma Stump took a swig straight from the rum bottle. 'In cash?'

Mr Canary nodded his agreement.

'Call it guineas and you got yerself a deal.'

Fin was so shocked her legs gave way and she slumped down beside the rocking chair. 'But, Ma!' she pleaded.

'Don't call me that!' Ma Stump took another swig from the rum bottle. 'I ain't your ma.'

6

Just then, there was a sharp rap at the door. Small darted over, but rather than barking and growling as usual, he sat, tongue hanging out, as if someone had just offered him a sausage.

Ma tutted. 'What now? George! Go and see who it is . . . and tell 'em to come back in the morning.'

But as soon as George opened the door, Lady Worth swept in.

'Who the devil are you?' Ma said.

'My name is Lady Worth . . . and you must be Ma Stump.' She looked around the poor damp attic, taking in Fin's tear-stained face, the apothecary in the armchair. 'Mr Canary? I didn't expect to find *you* here. What on earth is going on?'

Mr Canary's mouth opened and closed a few times, but no actual words came forth and it was left to Fin to explain. 'Ma's selling me to this rat-faced weasel as an apprentice, that's what.'

Ma reached out to give Fin a swipe, but Fin had sensibly positioned herself out of range. 'If you must know,' Ma said, 'we're doing a bit of business here, not that it's any of *yours*.'

'On the contrary. The welfare of this girl is very much my business,' Lady Worth replied.

Fin was baffled. What could she mean? Fin had scoffed down a pie with the lady, and answered what felt like a hundred questions, but other than that there was no connection between them at all.

Ma was just as doubtful. 'Oh yeah?' she sneered. 'And how d'you make that out?'

'I have come here to tell you –' Lady Worth locked eyes with Fin and took a deep breath – 'that this child is Magdalena, my long-lost niece.'

'You what? . . . You mean . . . you're my *aunty*?'

Lady Worth flinched at the familiar term. 'Indeed I am.'

'But . . . but what about my mum and dad?' Fin said.

Lady Worth frowned and looked at the floor. 'I'm sorry to tell you that my sister and her husband both passed away many years ago.'

Fin didn't know what to think. Was it some kind of joke? Instinctively, she looked at George, suspecting one of his horrible tricks, but George was no actor and he was blinking at Lady Worth, as surprised as anyone.

Ma tittered nastily. 'Come off it! How could you know? There's *'undreds* like her abandoned every minute of every day.'

'There can be no doubt, I assure you,' Lady Worth said. 'I have questioned the girl. Her age and situation are a match.'

Ma narrowed her eyes. 'So you says, but why should we take your word for it?'

'Do you really imagine that I would *pretend* to be related to this child?' Lady Worth's haughty gaze came to rest on Fin and the look of disgust on her face amply illustrated her words.

Fin huffed in indignation. No one had asked the lady to come. What was she doing here anyway, since she clearly found Fin so repulsive?

'Naturally,' Lady Worth continued, 'I am appalled by the connection, but I am afraid there is no denying it.'

'Then why don't you prove it?' Ma got out of the rocking chair and drew herself up. She'd been a bare-knuckle boxer in her youth, and still looked like someone who knew how to win a fight.

But Lady Worth was not to be intimidated. She lifted her chin. 'Very well. If you insist.' She tugged off one of her fur-trimmed gloves and held up her hand. There was a general gasp from the assembled company.

Like Fin, Lady Worth had an extra finger on her right hand. 'As you see, the girl is clearly a member of my family.'

A hush fell over the gathering and the only sound was the creak of the rocking chair as it slowed to a halt.

It must have been the thought of Mr Canary's five-and-twenty guineas slipping through her fingers, because suddenly Ma decided Fin was family after all.

'I'm not havin' it,' she said. 'She was left on *my* doorstep as a babber. She belongs to *me*.'

Fin had been watching this to-and-fro in a daze, but Ma's declaration brought her back to her senses. 'Shut up, all of you! You can stop your arguing, cos I don't belong to anyone.'

Lady Worth looked surprised, but after a moment she nodded. 'The girl's right. She's old enough to decide for herself.' She turned to Fin. 'You can come with me now, or you can go with Mr Canary. The choice is yours.'

There was a crack of thunder from outside. A second later, rain started hammering on the tiles, and then came the irregular plink of drips falling into the various jars and enamel bowls that had been placed under the leaks in the roof.

Fin looked from Lady Worth to Mr Canary, who was doing his best to give her an encouraging smile. She didn't trust either of them, but of the two she could tell which one Small preferred, and he was never wrong. On top of that, the lady offered the chance of finding out about her parents, a chance that no foundling could pass up.

'I'll go with the lady,' Fin announced.

'Ooh, you little turncoat! We're the ones what looked out for you all this time,' Ma said, gesturing to herself and George. 'We're yer family, not 'er!'

Fin went and stood next to Lady Worth. 'That's not what you said when you sold me out for twenty-five guineas just now.'

'Well that's settled then,' Lady Worth said. From her tone it was hard to say whether she cared one way or the other.

'Oh no you don't!' Ma dug her meaty fists into her hips. 'You can't come in 'ere and steal my girl. I'll have the bobbies on you . . . I'll –'

'You will do no such thing,' Lady Worth replied calmly. She drew a purse from her pocket and threw it to Ma. 'This will compensate you for your trouble.'

Then she turned to Fin. 'My carriage is outside. I shall wait downstairs while you make your goodbyes.'

Now that hard cash had exchanged hands, everyone seemed delighted. Ma went off into a corner to count her money, and George took advantage of the distraction, gulping down the contents of the rum bottle while her back was turned. Only Mr Canary was put out. He scrambled up from the armchair and stalked off without saying a word.

Fin took a final look around. Since their furniture got nicked, there wasn't much left: only the two chairs and a sorry pile of blankets in the corner where the three foundlings slept. Ma's attic was a dank, unhealthy place to call home, but it was the only one Fin had ever known, and it was a darn sight better than the workhouse next door.

'Well . . .' she said. 'Bye then.'

George held the rum bottle aloft and burped. 'Cheers, Fingers. Been nice knowin' ya.'

Ma said nothing. She was still intent on counting her money, and the only sound that came from her corner was the clink of coin.

'Ma?' Fin said. 'Ain't you got nothing at all to say to me before I go?'

No response was forthcoming, and Fin was about to give up when Ma held out her hand. 'Where's them ten shillings for the leeches?'

Fin sighed. She handed over the money and scooped Small into her arms. 'Come on,' she murmured into his fur, 'we're done here.' She turned and went out of the door.

On the stairs she bumped into Snot, soaked by the rain and hurrying up with a bottle of stout in his hand.

'Where you goin'?' He gestured to the carriage at the bottom of the steps. 'And who's that?'

'Ma was tryin' to sell me to Mr Canary, only she got a better offer.' Fin nodded towards the carriage. 'That lady says she's my aunty, and I got to go and live with her.'

Snot went pale. 'What about your mum and dad?'

Fin hung her head. 'Dead.'

'Oh.' Snot put down the stout and gave Fin a damp hug.

'I don't want to go,' Fin said. 'I'd much rather stay here with you.'

Snot pulled away and Fin could tell by the way his lip trembled that he was trying not to cry. 'No. That wouldn't be right,' he said bravely. 'You can't pass up an opportunity like this.' He picked the bottle up again and went past her up the steps. Only, before he disappeared inside, he turned back.

'Good luck, Fin.'

His eyes were wet, but whether he'd lost the battle with his tears or with the falling rain, it was impossible to tell.

A t the bottom of the stairs, Fin turned and looked back up towards the attic, the cruel words ringing in her head.

I ain't your ma.

What Ma said was no secret, but Fin had always believed she meant something more to the woman who had taken her in and brought her up. She'd believed Ma all those times she'd said Fin was like a daughter to her. Even now, Fin half expected Ma to appear in the doorway and call her back.

'Come along, Magdalena!'

Magdalena? It took a moment for Fin to realize the voice was Lady Worth's, and that she meant *her*.

It was too much to take in. But one thing was for certain – Ma had been right all along. Her parents would never be coming to fetch her.

She turned towards the carriage. On the door was a curious emblem which Fin guessed must be the family crest. It was a shield, with mountains and a full moon painted in the background, and in the middle, two six-fingered hands, crossed at the wrist, their little fingers locked together. At the bottom of the shield was a dog that looked a lot like Small.

'At least we're in this together,' Fin said, giving him a squeeze.

'Magdalena! Will you please hurry up!'

She climbed up into the carriage and sat down. 'The name's Fin.'

'Don't be ridiculous.' Lady Worth gave her a sour look. 'And that is not the gratitude one might expect.'

Here we go, typical posh, Fin thought. The lady had just turned Fin's life upside down and trampled the few good bits underfoot, but she wouldn't be satisfied until she got thanked for it.

'Gratitude for what?' Fin said.

'For saving you from that awful, damp attic, for one thing.'

'It was my home.'

'Home?' Lady Worth wrinkled her nose.

Fin thought about Ma and Snot and George, their constant teasing and cruelties. But also, sometimes, their unexpected kindnesses. She'd rarely gone without supper, and George and Snot usually let her sleep on the straw pallet, even if it was down the bottom by their stinky feet. 'I had a place there,' she said. 'I knew where I was. And I knew *who* I was. But now . . .'

'Well, now you have a new life and a new place, which I can assure you is far superior to Ma Stump's attic.'

'So where's that? Where we going?'

'Castle Kaminski.'

'Castle *Kaminski*? But I thought your name was Lady Worth!'

Even in the dim light of the carriage, Fin saw her blush, and when she answered her voice had none of its usual self-righteousness. 'I took my husband's name when I married,' she said.

'So you was once a Kaminski, then? That's the family name?'

Lady Worth huffed in annoyance. 'Yes, I used to be a Kaminski.'

'Kaminski ain't an English name though, is it?'

'No.' She was so abrupt, Fin thought she didn't mean to say any more, but after a moment she sighed and said, 'Our mother brought the family here from Poland more than twenty-five years ago.'

'Poland!' Fin cried, and she let out a long whistle. She could see that Lady Worth resented her questions. She seemed agitated, constantly wringing her hands, the extra finger she'd revealed now hidden inside her glove. Fin knew it was rude to keep asking, but if she could just learn something about her new situation, if she could understand it, then she might be able to damp down her nerves. Anyway, the lady had shown no concern for Fin's feelings with her endless prying questions back in the dining room of the pub . . .

Fin's mind went back to the Tripe and Eel, the lady's gasp and the look of horror on her face when she'd spotted Fin's hand. Fin realized now what that look was really about.

'You knew who I was soon as you spotted my fingers, didn't you?' she said.

'Well yes, I suppose so.'

'Then why didn't you say something straight away?'

Lady Worth pressed her lips together and looked out of the window. 'It was the shock.'

'Shock?' Fin shook her head. 'You just didn't want it to be true, did you?'

Her aunt turned on her. 'Can you blame me? Is it really beyond your imagination to understand my feelings? My sister was graceful, beautiful, well bred.' She stared off into the distance. 'Her deportment was exemplary and her manners were flawless.' The wistful look disappeared from Lady Worth's face and her cold eye came to rest again on Fin. 'How do you think it felt, to discover that *you*, a filthy street urchin, were my beloved sister's lost child?'

Fin would have liked to bite back, to ask her aunt if it was beyond *her* imagination to understand that she, Fin, had had a shock too. After all, she'd just learned that both her parents were dead and she had been an orphan all this time. But as far as Fin was concerned, Lady Worth's frosty manner was further proof that the sympathy of rich ladies and gentlemen did not extend beyond themselves and others like them. Fin would have been quite happy never to speak to her aunt again . . . only she desperately wanted answers about her parents.

'So what happened to my mum and dad?'

'I do not wish to speak of it.'

'I've got a right to know.'

'All in good time,' Lady Worth snapped.

Fin folded her arms across her chest. 'Yeah, cos I've only been waiting eleven years to find out.'

Lady Worth huffed. 'Very well then. If you must know, your father, and my husband alongside him, died in a road accident before you were born. Your mother . . . my beloved sister Marta –' she pressed her eyes shut and drew in a deep breath – 'she drowned.'

'Drowned?' Fin felt the blood drain from her face. 'But how?'

'I don't know.'

'Where?'

'I don't wish to discuss it. Can't you see how painful this is for me?'

But Fin needed to know. 'Then what happened? How did I end up on Ma Stump's doorstep?'

'Enough!' Lady Worth slammed her hand against the wall of the carriage. 'How could I possibly know the answer to that? We all thought you had drowned along with my poor sister, and perhaps it would've been better for everyone if –' She stopped herself, but it didn't take a genius to work out what had been coming next.

'If that's the way you feel,' Fin said, 'why bother claiming me at all?'

'I made a promise . . . one I now deeply regret.'

After that they travelled in silence, the only sound the drumming of the rain on the roof of the carriage. Fin wondered what kind of promise her aunt had made, but after everything she had learned so far that night, she didn't have the heart to ask. It was a horrible thing to know she was only there because the lady thought it her *duty*. Back at the attic, she might not have been wanted exactly, but at least she was useful. She allowed herself to think fondly of Snot and even George. Even

Ma's betrayal already seemed less terrible, and just the sort of thing that might happen when she'd had one too many.

The next few hours passed with Fin stroking Small's soft ears and anxiously wondering what lay ahead, and Lady Worth studiously looking out of the window, although once the street lamps of London had been left behind, it was pitch-dark and there was nothing to see.

At last, the rocking of the carriage lulled Fin to sleep. When she woke it was still night.

'Where are we?' she asked.

'We've just come through Epping Forest,' Lady Worth replied. 'We're on the marshes now and only a few miles to go.'

Fin sat up and looked out of the window. The rain had stopped, and in the moonlight, she could see behind them the outline of a forest against the horizon, and winding ahead, the raised road that cut through the boggy land. It looked and smelled like home, and Fin's spirits rose; she had been ripped from the only life she knew, but at least she would not have to leave her beloved marshes behind.

It was late at night when the carriage finally reached the carved stone archway marking the entrance to the long drive that led to the house.

'There,' Lady Worth said, pointing out of the window. 'That's Castle Kaminski.'

It was the first building they'd seen for miles, a red-brick blip on the horizon, without so much as a hillock or tree around it to break the line of the wide starry sky. It seemed a desolate place to live, and Lady Worth explained that the castle had been built by Fin's grandmother when the family first came to England.

'Why did she build a castle, not a normal house?' Fin asked.

'Your grandmother was a nervous type. She liked to see who was coming.'

Small, who was getting old these days, had been curled up asleep on Fin's lap for most of the journey, but now he stood with his forepaws on the windowsill, ears alert, eyes fixed on the approaching house.

'That's our new home,' Fin whispered to him.

'Hardly new,' Lady Worth said. 'He used to live here, as did you yourself.'

As they drew near, Fin began to appreciate the looming presence of the house, which seemed to have sprouted from the flat landscape like a gigantic mushroom. It was five storeys high and had been built on a slight rise so that it towered over the surrounding countryside. Despite its size, it wasn't much like a castle; it had no battlements or turrets, and the windows were as large as any Fin had seen in London. But then the carriage crossed a bridge and Fin saw that the house was surrounded by a moat, although as far as she could tell it had no water in it.

They drew up in front of the house and the footman jumped down from the back of the carriage. He pulled out the steps and helped Lady Worth climb down. 'Come along,' she said when Fin hung back.

To Fin's annoyance, Small showed no such reluctance. He leaped from the carriage and trotted towards the house, only stopping to sniff at the middle-aged woman in a plain, high-collared dress, who came hurrying down the steps to meet them.

'Good evening, madam,' she said. 'You're so late, we were starting to worry –' The woman stopped short when she saw Fin climbing down from the carriage.

'Good evening, Mrs Benton. This is . . . Fin,' Lady Worth said. 'Fin, this is Mrs Benton, our housekeeper.' She leaned towards the housekeeper and muttered, 'Take her in and have her scrubbed clean.'

'Very good, madam.' Mrs Benton looked Fin up and down warily. 'Come with me.'

She led Fin to a side door and into the kitchens, where two girls in neat grey pinafores and mob caps were washing a huge pile of dirty plates and dishes. 'Molly! Lizzy!' the housekeeper said. 'Get the bath out!'

'No need to bother on my account,' Fin said, but nobody was listening. She watched with mounting unease as the girls hauled in an enamel tub and filled it with hot water from a pot that had been hanging over the fire.

'Right,' Mrs Benton said as she turned to Fin, a block of pea-green carbolic soap in one hand and a scrubbing brush in the other. 'Strip those filthy clothes off and get in.'

Fin shook her head. 'You'll have my skin off with that carbolic. Anyways, I already had a bath.'

Mrs Benton raised an eyebrow. 'Oh, did you now? Last year was it?'

Molly and Lizzy sniggered at this, but Fin ignored them. 'No, it was only yesterday actually . . .' Mrs Benton advanced with the soap and Fin took a step backwards. 'I were out leeching, water up to me armpits. You ask Lady Worth if you don't believe me.'

Mrs Benton raised the scrubbing brush and narrowed her eyes. 'If you don't get those filthy rags off right now . . .'

Fin tried to dodge past, but the housekeeper got hold of one arm and Molly and Lizzy grabbed the other.

'Oy! Get off me!' Fin twisted about, but there was no escape. The three of them dumped her in the tub and set about her with stiff brushes and soap.

'The water's too hot!' she shouted, but no one paid the slightest attention. And there was worse to come when Mrs Benton insisted on washing her hair. Fin squirmed and fought, but Molly and Lizzy pinned her in place while the housekeeper lathered her long hair with soap. Rivulets of carbolic foam streamed down her face, stinging her eyes worse than any lime.

'Ow! You've blinded me!' Fin hollered as Molly emptied another pan of hot water over her head.

'Well,' Mrs Benton said, 'I wouldn't have guessed her hair was *red* in a month of Sundays. It looked black under all that grime.'

Molly got hold of one of Fin's hands. 'That's nothing, Mrs Benton. Would you look at the dirt under them nails!'

Lizzy grabbed at the other hand. 'Hang on, she's got an extra finger.'

Instantly, all three of them stopped lathering and scrubbing and went quiet.

'Well I never,' Mrs Benton said. 'After all these years . . . who'd have thought it? Now, Lizzy, now, Molly, you two just carry on here washing and rinsing, and mind you don't spill bathwater all over the floor.' She went off and came back with a pair of scissors and cut Fin's nails, including her especially long one.

'Ow! You can't do that!' Fin said. 'What am I supposed to peel them leeches off with now?'

Mrs Benton shook her head. 'You won't be going leeching any more, child.'

It was obvious really, but it still came to Fin as a shock. Her life really had changed forever.

At last the ordeal was over and Fin stood shivering in front of the fire, wrapped in a towel.

'Where's my clothes?' she said.

'Burned,' Mrs Benton informed her. 'But Madam sent this down for you.' She held out a satin-trimmed nightdress that was so fine it looked as if it had been made out of a cloud.

Fin felt her face flush with anger. Her clothes were little more than rags, but even so, they were *hers*. How dare they throw them on the fire without asking! But before she could open her mouth to complain, Fin was made to put her arms up and the nightdress was forced over her head.

'I'll only have to get changed again in the morning,' she muttered. 'What's wrong with going to bed in normal clothes?'

Mrs Benton handed her a cup of hot milk. 'Here, drink this,' she told her, and she watched her gulp it down. 'Now, off to bed. Follow me.'

The housekeeper lit an oil lamp and led the way up a plain wooden staircase off the kitchens. Fin emerged, two floors up, into a different world. Here, the walls were covered in crimson flock wallpaper with tasselled swags of silk and oil paintings in gold frames. The floorboards were highly polished, reflecting the light of the chandeliers that hung from the ceilings, ablaze with candles. Fin was afraid to touch anything. No wonder Lady Worth had been unimpressed by the dining room at the Tripe and Eel.

Mrs Benton opened a door at the end of the corridor and Fin followed her inside. 'This is your room,' the housekeeper said.

Fin couldn't believe it. The space was twice the size of Ma Stump's attic and even in the poor light of the oil lamp she could see how rich it was. There were silk curtains at the window and the wallpaper had a design of repeating images of trees and birds and flowers. Fin went over to the bed, which had a canopy of ruched pink velvet suspended above it. 'Blimey,' she said.

'What's the matter?' Mrs Benton said. 'Don't you like it?'

'No, it's just . . . I ain't never slept in a bed before.'

'Well, I'm sure you'll get used to it.' Mrs Benton put the lamp down on the bedside table, pulled back the sheets and Fin got in. 'There now, settle yourself down and I'll bid you goodnight.'

'Mrs Benton?' Fin said. 'Can I ask you something?'

'Certainly you can.'

'Did you know my mum?'

Mrs Benton looked taken aback by the question, but after a moment she nodded and even smiled. 'Of course I did. I have been housekeeper here for more than twenty years.'

'What d'you think happened to her?'

'Now that I really couldn't say.'

The door had been left ajar and as they were talking, Small trotted in. He patrolled the edges of the room, whining and growling and sniffing in all the corners. Fin called to him and he jumped up on to the bed.

'Get down, Hercules,' Mrs Benton said. 'I'll find you a place in front of the kitchen fire.'

'*Hercules?*' Fin said.

'That's his name.'

'No!' Fin put her arm round him. They could take her clothes, but they weren't getting their hands on her dog – or his name. 'He's called Small,' she said, 'and he always sleeps with me.'

Mrs Benton sighed. 'All right then, seeing as it's your first night. Now I must be getting on. Goodnight, miss.'

When the housekeeper had gone, Small leaped down and paced back and forth in front of the door, snuffling at the air.

'What's the matter, Small?' Fin said. 'Why you acting all protective?' But Fin felt just as uneasy. As she lay in bed, her gaze traced the coiling pattern on the paper that covered the walls. Rainbow-coloured birds of paradise perched in the branches of vines, and the vines intertwined with flowers whose petals were edged in silver and gold. It was all wondrous and beautiful, but despite the opulence, the pristine, polished surfaces, there was a strange atmosphere in the house. Something that pressed in on Fin. Something that seemed to suck the energy out of the air and made it hard to get her breath.

She called to Small and he jumped back up on to the bed and curled up next to her. He shut his eyes, but his ears stayed alert and twitched at every distant sound.

Fin lay back, tired out, but how could she sleep after all that had happened over the course of the day? She'd got up that morning a leecher, and now she was . . . what? A lady? Hardly!

It was the last thing Fin had expected. She'd always assumed her mother was too poor to keep and feed a child. Like Ma said, it happened all the time. Women left their babies all over London. Not because they wanted to, but because they had no choice. Every abandoned baby's story was a sad story, but at least they made some sense. *But mine doesn't,* Fin thought. *My mother was called Marta, and she was rich, and yet she left me as a baby wrapped in nothing but newspaper on the doorstep of a stranger, and shortly after that she drowned.* Fin couldn't help feeling that this version of her story didn't make any sense at all.

'Thank goodness you're here,' she whispered to Small, who opened one eye and licked her nose.

Fin turned over, determined to stop worrying about it and get some sleep. She had nothing to complain about. The bed was snug and the pillows were soft – in fact, she had never been so warm and comfortable – but again her thoughts went back to the attic . . . How she wished she was there with the people she'd known all her life!

By now, she'd worked up an excuse for what Ma Stump had done. Fin put aside the fact that money had changed hands and told herself that Ma had only acted in what she thought were Fin's best interests. Mr Canary was a creep, but that wasn't Ma's fault, was it? And anyway, everyone knew an apprentice shop girl was a plum job.

The main thing was that she had *fitted in* at Ma's attic, which made up for a lot.

Fin thought ruefully how she used to moan about the stink, about George's fidgeting, Snot's snoring, the calls of the bargemen on the river, the cries and moans from the workhouse next door. Here it was *too* quiet, and Fin realized she had never been without human company at night before. She found herself listening for any sign of life in the darkness, but all she could hear were the creaks and groans of the house, which, not being human sounds, gave her no comfort at all.

9

Fin was woken late the next morning by Molly bringing in her breakfast on a tray. 'Mrs Benton said you'd be tired and to leave you be so you could sleep, so I'm afraid you've missed breakfast with the family.'

'Family?' Fin said, rubbing her eyes.

'Yes. Your cousin, Miss Emily, came downstairs specially. She was most put out when you didn't appear, and Master Eryk is also anxious to meet you.' Molly leaned towards Fin and whispered, 'He's your second cousin, from Poland, and an orphan after both his parents were taken by typhoid less than a year ago.'

Lizzy bustled in carrying an armful of clothes, which she laid on the bed. 'Some of Miss Emily's clothes for you,' she said. 'Only, Mrs Benton said not to get dressed yet cos the seamstress is here . . .'

By the time Fin had been measured for new clothes and hats and shoes, and Mrs Benton had chosen fabrics from the seamstress's swatches, the afternoon was gone.

'It's hardly worth your while putting a day dress on,' the housekeeper said, 'so we may as well get you dressed ready for dinner. Here –' she held out an armful of lacy white undergarments that smelled of lavender and rose water – 'put these on.'

'Ain't never bothered with this flim-flam before,' Fin muttered as she struggled into a pair of drawers, followed by a satin-trimmed chemise, and then not one but two flannel petticoats.

Once the underwear was on, Mrs Benton held up a dress. It was made of midnight-blue velvet with a bow at the waist and a lace trim at the neck and wrists.

'I can't wear that,' Fin said, taken aback.

Mrs Benton tutted. 'You want to sit down to dinner in your drawers?'

Fin rubbed the sumptuous fabric between her fingers. 'But it's too good. I'll get it dirty.'

Mrs Benton sighed. 'Then we'll clean it, won't we?' She sat Fin down at the dressing table and called Molly over to arrange her hair. 'Give it a really good brush, and then I think a centre parting with a blue ribbon would look perfect.'

It took a long time to get eleven years' worth of tangles out, and there were a few stubborn clumps that had to be cut off with scissors. With every sweep of the hairbrush, Fin let out an indignant yelp. 'Is this going to happen every day?' she moaned.

'It won't be nearly so bad next time,' Molly said, tying an enormous bow on the top of Fin's head. She put her hand under Fin's chin and gently raised her face towards the mirror. 'There now. See how well you look? If it weren't for the scowl, you'd look a proper lady.'

Fin lifted her eyes to her reflection. Molly was right, she could hardly recognize the girl in the mirror. She had the uncomfortable feeling that she was an impostor who shouldn't be there at all.

Once Molly had finished, Mrs Benton took over again. She fussed about, retying the velvet bow at Fin's waist and smoothing the hem of her dress. Finally she was satisfied and stood back to take in the effect. 'Well, if I do say so myself, you certainly look the part.'

Fin attempted a smile. She might look 'the part' but she didn't feel it. However much they prettied her up on the outside, on the inside she was still Fin – a poor foundling whose only education was in the best way to catch a leech. As soon as she opened her mouth, everyone would know who she really was.

Just then, Small trotted in. He came to a sudden halt when he saw Fin and put his head on one side as if confused.

'It's me, you idiot,' Fin said, holding out her hand for Small to sniff at. 'I might look weird, but it's still just me.'

Mrs Benton waved Small away. 'Time for dinner,' she said. 'The family are gathering in the dining room.'

The housekeeper led Fin downstairs. They went along a corridor lined with tall, elegant windows, and stopped outside a pair of mahogany doors that were each painted with the six-fingered hands that Fin had seen on the door of the carriage. Lady Worth looked and behaved nothing like Fin, but here was the one small thing they had in common. It had marked her out as one of them.

Mrs Benton turned to give Fin a final once-over. 'Mind your manners,' she said, picking a loose thread from Fin's sleeve. 'No cursing, and only speak when spoken to.'

The housekeeper knocked on the door and, a moment later, Lady Worth came out. She looked Fin up and down. 'Good job, Mrs Benton. That's quite a transformation.' Mrs Benton inclined her head in acknowledgement, then bustled away back down the corridor.

'Now,' Lady Worth said as she took hold of Fin's elbow and guided her through the double doors. 'Come along with me and meet your cousins.'

Fin had never seen such a grand room. A twelve-armed chandelier hung over the table, its brilliant light doubled by the giant gilt mirror above the fireplace. The glare was further multiplied and broken into a thousand shining points by the glint of the crystal wine glasses, the whiteness of the linens, the sparkle of the silver cutlery.

'Blimey!' Fin said, despite Mrs Benton's warning to remain silent.

Lady Worth ignored the outburst and led her to the table. 'This is my daughter, Emily.'

Emily was a thin, pale girl. She held out a limp six-fingered hand for Fin to shake and smiled at her kindly. 'I'm very much looking forward to getting to know you, Cousin,' she said.

Next, Lady Worth steered Fin towards a man with a handlebar moustache and greased whiskers who sat at the head of the table, and whose narrowed eyes had followed Fin from the moment she came into the room. When she stood before him, he neither offered his hand nor smiled. He only raised his chin and, although Fin was standing and he was sitting, he still managed to look down his nose at her. 'Not *another* penniless relation?' he said to Lady Worth. 'First the Polish boy and now this one. Is there no end to these waifs and strays?'

Lady Worth didn't seem to notice the snub. 'This is Doctor Hunt, my daughter's physician.' She laid a hand on the doctor's shoulder. 'He's been a godsend, and I don't know what we would do without him. We are so very grateful to the good doctor, aren't we, Emily?'

Emily smiled blandly. 'Yes, Mama.'

Just then, the door sprang open and a tall, dark-haired boy, about Fin's age, came bundling in. He was all trussed up in a starched collar and tweed suit.

Lady Worth turned a withering look on him. 'Eryk! How many times must I tell you? Dinner is served at six.'

'Yes indeed,' Dr Hunt said, nodding solemnly. 'Poor show.'

Eryk replied in a strong accent. 'I am very sorry –' Then he caught sight of Fin. His eyes widened and he said something in another language. This must be the Polish boy the doctor had mentioned.

Lady Worth gasped and her hand flew to her mouth. 'How dare you! I will not have this . . . this *superstition* in my house, and neither will I tolerate that ugly language!'

'Hear, hear,' Dr Hunt said, taking a gulp of wine from his glass. 'We're in England, man. Speak English!'

Fin wondered what the boy could have said to so upset Lady Worth.

Eryk himself didn't seem to be listening. For a moment, he continued to stare at Fin, mouth open, but then he recovered himself. He made a stiff bow and held out his hand to her. 'Is delight to make your acquaintance.'

Lady Worth showed Fin to a seat between Emily and Eryk. Now she could see that almost everything on the table carried the family emblem. There were six-fingered hands engraved on the crystal glasses, on the silver cutlery and on the china plates. It was even moulded into the plaster of the cornice in each corner of the ceiling.

Lady Worth rang a bell and Lizzy came in with a steaming tureen of delicious-smelling soup. Fin was starving, and as soon as she'd been served she lifted the bowl to her lips. There was a shocked intake of breath around the table and Fin looked up to find Lady Worth staring at her in horror. Dr Hunt smirked and muttered something to her behind his hand about 'savages'.

To Fin's embarrassment, Eryk found it all very funny. 'You must use spoon,' he said, not managing to smother his laughter behind his hand.

Fin shot him a filthy look and grabbed a spoon. But there were spoons of many different shapes and sizes laid out round Fin's placemat and it appeared she had chosen the wrong one. It took a few more seconds of dithering mortification, and help from Emily, before she finally settled on the correct spoon.

Fin heaved a sigh of relief, but it turned out this was only one of many complicated rules for the eating of soup. The spoon couldn't just be plunged into the middle of the bowl; for some nonsensical reason it had to be used to scoop soup from the side of the bowl that was *furthest away*. And there was to be no dipping of bread either, although you could take a bite of bread and *then* a spoonful of soup if you so wished. Most important of all, the soup had to be transferred from spoon to mouth silently. The way Lady Worth and Dr Hunt flinched at the smallest hint of a slurp told Fin it was considered a high crime.

When everyone had finished, Molly and Lizzy cleared the bowls and side plates away. But moments later they returned with platters piled with mounds of roasted meat and potatoes.

'What, there's more?' Fin said. The food looked and smelled delicious, but her heart sank as she realized this would mean another set of pointless rules.

By now she could hardly think straight, and Fin thought she had never felt so grateful when Emily tried to help. She didn't mock, but smiled her encouragement and picked up her own cutlery first, so Fin could copy the special grip she used, her index fingers hovering on top of the knife and fork in a way that looked most awkward.

Lady Worth averted her eyes from Fin's struggles, but Dr Hunt rudely watched her every move. He tutted loudly when a potato fell off Fin's fork and back on to her plate, splashing the front of her dress with gravy. This time, he didn't bother to whisper. 'You see? Didn't I say the girl would've been far better off apprenticed to Mr Canary?'

The food in Fin's mouth seemed suddenly too big to swallow. She grabbed for her glass, knocking water all over the tablecloth.

'What did I tell you?' the doctor said. 'A guttersnipe in velvet is still a guttersnipe.'

Fin felt the blood rush to her face. Not caring what anyone thought, she spat her mouthful of food back on to the plate. 'You know what?' she said. 'I've done my best for you lot, but I'd rather starve than be forced to pick at my food with these!' She waved her hand, taking in the whole ridiculous array of knives and forks and spoons that surrounded her. 'Instruments o' torture, that's what they is!'

With that, Fin stormed out of the dining room and upstairs to her bedroom. Once there, she pulled off the restrictive velvet dress, tore the stupid ribbon out of her hair, and kicked the whole lot into the corner before flinging herself down on the bed. Small had been curled up on the armchair by the window, but seeing her distress he trotted over, jumped up on to the bed and pushed his head under her arm.

'They don't want me,' she said to him. 'Why did they ever bring me here?'

Fin was well used to hard knocks. Where she came from, everyone was expected to take a ribbing and Fin knew how to give back as good as she got. But the loathing twisted up inside Dr Hunt's sneering superiority was something different. It hurt far more than any of the casual insults she'd had from Ma and Snot and George. Maybe, Fin thought, it got under her skin because it was the truth. She didn't belong here. Hadn't she looked in the mirror and thought the same herself?

Not for the first time, Fin wished she was back home. It hadn't been so bad, and as Ma often pointed out, there were worse places to be, like the workhouse next door where the children were so thin, Ma said, you could see sunlight through them on a bright day.

There was a tentative knock and Emily poked her head round the door. 'Fin?'

When Fin didn't say anything, Emily came over and sat down on the edge of the bed.

Fin turned her face away so Emily wouldn't see she'd been crying. 'What d'you want?'

'To apologize. What Doctor Hunt said was awful.' There was a loud creak from the corridor outside and Emily glanced nervously over her shoulder. 'I shouldn't really be here. I told Mama I was going straight to bed, but I couldn't let you think I agree with anything the doctor said.'

Fin sat up. 'Lady Worth seems to like him.'

Emily nodded thoughtfully. 'She thinks the world of him . . . and I suppose I ought to be grateful. Mama says I'm so much better since I've been under his care.'

Fin glanced at Emily's face. She was so pale that Fin could see the blue veins under the skin round her eyes. 'Do *you* think you're better?'

Emily was quiet for a moment, then she shrugged. 'I've been ill for such a long time. I can't remember. But let's not talk about that now.' She leaned over and took Fin's hand. 'Do you know, we're almost the same age? If things had been different, we would've grown up together, like sisters –' She stopped at the sound of voices coming from the stairwell outside. 'I'd better go,' she said, squeezing Fin's hand. 'The doctor says I've had too much excitement and I'm to spend at least the next week in bed. Promise you'll come and see me?'

When Emily had gone, Fin wondered how things might have been if her mother had lived and she had grown up here, in this grand house. Would she have ended up as nervous and downtrodden as Emily? She remembered the way Lady Worth had described Fin's mother to her, referring to her breeding, her exemplary deportment and flawless manners. She'd made Fin's mother sound as cold and precise as Lady Worth herself – a selfish, upper-class toff. In other words, the sort of person Fin had learned to hate.

It was a horrible thought. None of the things Fin had recently been told about her mother matched the treasured image she had always held on to in her mind. She didn't want to believe her mother had willingly abandoned her, and she certainly didn't want to believe she could have been anything like Lady Worth.

The next morning, Fin waited until it was quite late before going down for breakfast. She didn't feel up to any fresh confrontations with the family, and she was relieved to find the dining room empty but the breakfast dishes still laid out. She took two plates and was serving herself and Small cold scrambled eggs when someone cleared their throat. 'I knew you will eventually appear – everyone must eat.' It was Eryk, half hidden behind the curtain in the window seat. 'I have been waiting.'

'What for?' Fin plonked herself down at the table, making sure her back was towards him.

But Eryk came over and sat facing her. 'I am wanting to get to know you.'

Fin eyed him suspiciously. 'Why?'

'You are my second cousin,' Eryk held up his six-fingered hand. 'A Kaminski.'

Fin stuffed a forkful of scrambled eggs into her mouth. 'Oh that,' she said, deliberately speaking with her mouth full. 'Don't I disgust you with my guttersnipe ways?'

In answer, he snatched her fork out of her hand, scooped some of Fin's food into his mouth, chewed, and then stuck his tongue out with all the bits of egg still stuck to it.

Fin ducked her head to hide her smile. 'Anyways, what d'you want?'

He stood up and bowed, as he had done the night before. 'I take you on tour of house.'

Small yipped in agreement and Eryk leaned down and patted him on the head. 'I like Small. He is clever dog.'

It hadn't escaped Fin's notice that Small seemed to tolerate Eryk well enough too, and he was never wrong about who could be trusted. Maybe Eryk wasn't so bad. After all, he had tried to help her manage the cutlery at dinner the night before, even if he had laughed at her mistakes. In many ways, he was in the same boat as Fin. Molly had said he was an orphan, and Dr Hunt had referred to him as 'penniless', so maybe he too was stuck here, having to be grateful for Lady Worth's charity because he had nowhere else to go.

'All right,' Fin said. 'But let's start outside. I want to get some fresh air out on the marshes.'

'Oh no you don't!' came a firm voice. It was Mrs Benton, who had come in with Molly to clear the dishes. 'Lady Worth has made it quite clear that no one is to go beyond the gardens.'

'But why?' Fin said.

'Quicksand, of course! That marshland is dangerous, and the doctor says the miasmas are bad for children's lungs.'

Fin laughed in disbelief. 'But I worked there! I were practically *born* on the marshes.'

But Mrs Benton would not budge. She said that Fin had *not* been born on the marshes; that, actually, she'd been born at Castle Kaminski, and that she would do well to put her gallivanting aside and start learning how to behave like a lady.

Outside was just as Fin had imagined. Neatly pruned rose bushes were arranged in rows, imprisoned behind clipped box hedges, and there was a lawn so trim and tidy it looked as if the garden had been carpeted.

Fin stood with Eryk, gazing out beyond the orderly flower beds towards the wild marshland. She longed to escape there, to get away from the confines of Castle Kaminski.

Eryk turned to her. 'You say to Mrs Benton you work on marshes . . . Why don't you go to school?'

'There weren't no time for all that.' Fin dug her hands into her hips in imitation of Ma. '*Don't earn, don't eat.*'

'Then what work you do?'

'I were a leecher.' She went on to describe the finer points of catching the slimy worms. She explained the importance of letting the leech have its fill of blood, else it would spit poison back into you. 'Which is how,' Fin told him, 'Ma's own grandma lost her leg.'

Eryk looked horrified and changed the subject. 'You miss London?'

Fin only nodded, but the mention of her previous home brought back the vivid sights, sounds and smells of Hackney. She missed it so much, it made her feel sick. 'What about you? Ain't you homesick?'

'Very much. I come from mountains, and I am not used to this flatness everywhere.' (So Fin had guessed right – like her, Eryk would much rather be somewhere else.) He looked down at his feet. 'But mostly, it is my parents I miss.'

It began to rain, and they went back inside the house. As Eryk showed her around, Fin saw that no expense had been spared on the furnishings. There was no shortage of space either, and the castle had a room for everything. There was a library, a study, a billiard room, a gun room, a room for the morning and another one for the afternoon. There were any number of bedrooms, along with spare rooms and guest rooms and rooms named after every colour in the rainbow. This dizzying multitude was spread across five floors, with many staircases, both straight and spiral, in between, and every room and corridor as neat and buttoned-up as Lady Worth herself.

They ended the tour back up on the top floor of the house and stood together, looking out of the window at all the wide-open space that was denied to them. From here, Fin could see to the dark line of the birch forest that cut across the marshes and, beyond that, faraway in the distance, the smog hovering over London. She sighed and turned away.

'You don't like house?' Eryk said.

Fin shrugged. 'It's very . . . nice.'

'But?'

'I thought I might find something of my mum and dad here, but there's nothing. The whole place feels . . . I dunno . . . soulless.'

Eryk nodded. 'Your aunt does not like reminder of past.'

'I've noticed.'

'Wait here,' Eryk said. 'I have idea.'

He was gone so long Fin was starting to think he'd forgotten about her, but then he returned with an oil lamp and a big smile on his face.

'What you lookin' so smug about?' Fin said.

'I speak to Mrs Benton. She say to look in attic.'

So, from the top-floor landing, they went up the narrow staircase that led to the door of the attic. Fin wrinkled her nose at the smell of damp; it reminded her of Ma Stump's.

Eryk tried the handle. 'Is locked.'

'How? There ain't no keyhole.' Fin stood back from the door and looked around her, then she pointed at the patches of black mould on the ceiling, the blown paint round the door frame. 'Wet's got in. I reckon the wood's swollen and it's stuck.'

Eryk passed Fin the oil lamp he was carrying. He put his shoulder against the door and, after a couple of shoves, it gave way, propelling him into the darkness of the room beyond. The whoosh of the opening door stirred up the thick layer of dust that lay on the floorboards, and Eryk coughed and flapped his hands. 'No person has walked here for years,' he said.

Fin followed him in. She lifted the lamp and their shadows crept across the floor and climbed the looming shapes hidden under bedsheets, the piles of boxes and crates stacked against the white-washed walls.

Suddenly, Small appeared. He trotted past them, his little paws making a trail in the unmarked dust. He sniffed at the air and sneezed before scampering to the other end of the narrow room, where he took hold of the corner of a sheet in his jaws. He began to walk backwards, growling and tugging, until he'd pulled the sheet off the thing hidden underneath. It was a rocking horse.

Fin went over to have a look. It was painted and gilded like the horses she'd seen on the merry-go-round at the fair. She set it rocking, then immediately wished she hadn't. The horse was only a toy, but with its staring eye and bared teeth it seemed full of menace as it plunged to and fro in the darkness.

She edged away and went to look at a crate Small was snuffling at. Inside, she found more children's toys packed in straw. She lifted out a spinning top, a bag of marbles, a china doll with yellow ringlets and a silk dress. Fin was about to pack them back in the straw when something shiny at the bottom of the box caught her eye. Picking it up and holding it close to the lamp, she saw that it was an old-fashioned tinderbox, like the one Ma kept for lighting the fire when she ran out of matches. Only this one was beautifully made from polished brass, and it was embellished with mountains and a pair of six-fingered hands, the family crest that she'd seen everywhere in the house. When she turned the box over, her heart sped up. A name, MARTA, was engraved on the back.

It was the first thing Fin had ever seen or touched of her mother's and tears gathered in her eyes. She wiped them away and carefully polished the tinderbox on her skirt. Then she cradled it in her hand, tracing the engraving of her mother's name with a finger. It proved she had really existed, that she had once lived in this house. The discovery left her feeling torn. On the one hand, Fin felt like an alien at Castle Kaminski, yet, on the other, here was an object, and a name, that tied her undeniably to this place and the family that lived here.

Eryk interrupted her thoughts. 'Come, look at this.'

Fin slipped the tinderbox into her pocket and crossed the room to see what he had found. It was a doll's house, a perfect copy of Castle Kaminski itself. The front of the miniature house was hinged and Eryk opened it out to reveal the rooms within. It was decorated like the real thing, with wallpaper and rugs, and tiny pieces of furniture. Behind the mahogany doors of the dining room, where Fin had eaten her dinner the night before, a family of tiny dolls sat round the table, with miniature cutlery and porcelain plates laid out in front of them. There was even a little Mrs Benton and a maid in the kitchen, where strands of yellow and red silk recreated the burning flames in the fireplace.

Fin brought the lamp a little closer. 'Look,' she said, pointing at one of the dolls at the dining table. 'I think that's meant to be Lady Worth.' Sitting next to her was a man-doll with a neat beard, who Fin guessed must be Lady Worth's husband. On the other side sat a small, dark-haired girl. 'That must be Emily,' Fin said.

Eryk shook his head. 'Emily is baby,' and he pointed to a tiny doll lying in a crib in the nursery.

Fin peered closer. 'Then who's the other girl?'

'Is cousin Penelope,' Eryk said. 'She was ill and died long time ago.'

A chill travelled up Fin's back. 'Then this doll's house must've been hers!' She stood up and closed the façade on the family that once was. It didn't feel right, poking through a dead girl's things. She looked around the attic, at all the things hidden in boxes or under sheets. No wonder. Lady Worth had lost her husband, her sister, and then her eldest daughter too. Who would want to be reminded of that? Fin thought about Emily, so delicate and pale. Perhaps she'd been too quick to judge the way Lady Worth fussed about her daughter's health.

She was about to suggest they go when Eryk called her over again. This time he'd found a stack of frames leaning against the wall, and he held up a sepia-toned photograph that had been touched up with coloured paints. 'This was taken near my village in Poland,' he said. 'On border with Transylvania.'

Fin could just make out the scene. There were snow-topped mountains all around, and in the foreground three smiling girls in puff-sleeved blouses, their heads garlanded with flowers. 'Look,' Eryk pointed to each girl in turn. 'That is Bashka . . . Lady Worth in middle . . . and this one –'

Fin snatched the picture from him and held it close to the flickering flame. She didn't need Eryk to tell her who the other girl was. 'I know,' Fin said. 'I . . . I recognize her.'

Eryk looked at Fin doubtfully. 'How is possible? You were baby when you were lost.'

Fin glared at him. 'I ain't lying! I've been dreaming about that face all my life.' She propped the picture up against the side of the crate and positioned the lamp so that a bright beam fell on her mother's face. Unlike Lady Worth, who even as a girl had been as neat as a pin, Marta looked more carefree. Her hair was dishevelled and her crown of flowers flopped over on one side. She did not look at all prim, as Lady Worth had described her. Her face was full of life, just as Fin remembered it. Fin felt such relief that a knot formed in her throat and she was afraid she would cry again.

'I do not say you are liar,' Eryk said. 'But this is one of many other strange things.'

'Strange? Like what?'

He gazed at her in the gloom, one eyebrow raised, as if trying to decide what to say. Eventually, he said, 'What do you know about our family, the Kaminskis?'

'Nothing.'

'Lady Worth must tell you something in carriage, no?'

Fin huffed. 'You're joking! She's like a clam, that one.'

He nodded. 'Is like I said before – she does not like to speak about past. That is why she hide behind her husband's English name. She does not like to remember old country or family history.'

'What history is that then?'

'There is book, *History of the Kaminskis*.' He hesitated before continuing, glancing to right and left as if afraid of being overheard. 'There is just one copy, many hundreds of years old, written by Kaminski ancestors . . .'

He stopped again and Fin couldn't bear the rising tension any longer. 'What?' she snapped. 'What does it say?'

He leaned in towards her, blocking out the lamplight, and the shadows that surrounded them seemed to lean in too. 'It say Kaminski family live under terrible curse.' His eyes darkened. 'It say our ancestor, Countess Kaminski . . . is *strzyga*.'

'"S trigger"?' Fin repeated. The strange word hung in the air between them. Fin had never heard it before, but the horrible tearing sound of it was enough to tell her something of what it meant.

'Yes, *strzyga*. Our ancestor, Countess Kaminski is *undead*. She is demon.' He glanced around the attic. 'I hope to find book, but is not here. But Polish legend say *strzygi* are born with two hearts; one they leave in grave, the other rise to live again.'

Eryk's statement was so blunt and unexpected that all Fin could do was stare at him. She expected him to nudge her at any moment and say he was joking, but he just blinked at her.

'What?' she said, when she finally found her voice. 'Undead like . . . like a vampire? Them ghouls what suck blood?'

Eryk shook his head. '*Strzygi* are not vampires. Is familiars of *strzyga* who feed on blood.'

'Familiars?'

'Yes, her companions. Some are living, others are living dead.'

Fin suddenly felt cold. If they'd been anywhere else, she would've laughed in Eryk's face, but in the gloom of the attic, surrounded by dead people's things, she couldn't even raise a smile. 'So what does a *strzyga* feed on then?'

Eryk narrowed his eyes. 'Different things, but this one, the Countess, she feed on memories of her own family's children.'

A demon countess that feeds on *memories?* It had to be a joke. Maybe he was getting her back for the gory details she'd revealed about her job as a leecher? But there was something in Eryk's voice that made Fin shiver.

'You're tryin' to scare me, ain't you?' she said. 'You jus' wanted to get me up here so you could tell me ghost stories, didn't you?' She lifted her chin. 'Well, I don't frighten easy, if that's what you think.'

Eryk looked taken aback. 'No, I do not do this. I tell you truth.'

Fin rolled her eyes. 'Come off it! I've never heard anything so ridiculous in me life!'

She kept expecting Eryk to laugh or apologize, but he continued to look deadly serious. 'You would not say this if you were born in my village. Everyone there knows truth about *them*, about undead. *Strzygi* feed at night and –'

'I ain't listening to no more of this.' Fin turned to go, but Eryk's hand reached out of the darkness and closed round her wrist.

'I believe Countess has travelled here, to England.'

Fin shook him off. 'Stop it, Eryk! It ain't funny no more.' She called Small to heel and hurried out.

She was halfway down the narrow staircase when she stopped, wondering if she should go back for the picture of the three sisters in the mountains. But she was too shaken up and annoyed with Eryk to go back. Anyway, she told herself, she didn't need it. She had the image of her mother's face perfectly remembered in her mind, and that had more life and meaning for Fin than any sepia photograph ever could.

That afternoon, Fin went to visit Emily, as she had promised.

Her cousin was in bed, propped up on a vast mound of pillows, as pale as a pig's trotter in dripping, but when she saw Fin, she managed a smile and called her over to her bedside.

'How are you feeling?' Fin asked.

'A little weak. Doctor Hunt says my humours are overheated.'

Fin was surprised. Emily's face was ashen and the last thing she looked was 'overheated'. 'What's the cure?' she said.

Emily rubbed at the bandage wrapped round her forearm. 'He says letting a cup of blood each day will help . . . but please let's not talk of that. Tell me what you've been up to instead.'

'Well, me and Eryk have been in the attic and found all sorts,' Fin said.

'How exciting!' A little colour came to Emily's cheeks. 'I don't think I've ever been up there. What did you find?'

'A picture of my mum, for one thing. It was when she was a kid, back in Poland, with your mum and Aunty Bashka.'

Emily's eyes widened. 'Ah yes, the infamous Aunty Bashka.'

'What d'you mean, "infamous"?'

Emily looked round, as if someone might be listening. 'Well, no one's seen her for years, and I'd forgotten I even had an aunty, but the other day I overheard Lizzy tell Molly that Aunty's involved in something quite disgraceful.'

'Like what?'

'Something to do with –' she leaned forward and whispered – '*the theatre.*'

'She an actress then?'

'Something like that. I asked Mama about it, but she got quite angry and has forbidden me from ever mentioning her name again.'

'Hmmm,' Fin said. 'Seems there's quite a few things Lady Worth don't like to talk about . . . Anyway, when I was in the attic, I found this.' She took the tinderbox out of her pocket and showed it to Emily.

'Oh! What a lovely thing,' she said, turning it over and peering at the engravings before handing it back. 'What else did you find?'

'Loads of toys. I expect some of them was yours. There was a rocking horse and a doll's house that used to belong to Penelope.'

Emily frowned. 'Penelope? Who's Penelope?'

'You know,' Fin said. 'Your sister.'

Emily blinked a few times. 'I don't have a sister.'

'Well, no.' Fin bit her lip. 'Not any more . . . She died, remember?'

For a moment, Emily stared, open-mouthed. Then she began to shake. 'Oh! I'm having one of my turns!'

Fin jumped up. 'I'll call the doctor.'

But Emily reached out a hand to stop her. 'Please don't. I'll be all right . . . really. Just pass me that glass of water, would you?' She took a few sips and looked fearfully into Fin's face. 'I don't remember her . . . I don't remember having a sister – and that's not something I should've forgotten, is it?'

Fin suddenly went cold. Emily's forgetfulness was uncomfortably like the ghoulish story Eryk had told to frighten her, but she forced a reassuring smile on to her face. 'Don't blame yourself,' she said. 'It's only cos you're ill.'

Emily clasped her hands together. 'Oh, Fin, I'm so afraid.'

'Afraid of what?'

'That I'll never get better. That I'll die, here in this room, in this bed.' She grabbed Fin's hand and squeezed it tightly. 'I have horrible dreams, terrible nightmares.'

Fin gazed at Emily's frightened face. When you were poor, like she was, it was easy to think that the rich weren't real people; and as Fin knew very well from experience, rich people did not usually see human beings in the poor. But poor or rich, Fin realized now, they all shared the same fears and frailties. When you got up close, everyone was much the same.

Fin patted Emily's hand. 'Try not to agitate yerself,' she said. 'It'll be all right. We all have nasty dreams sometimes, but they ain't real.'

'That's what the doctor says. But they *feel* so real, and sometimes I think someone really does come into my room at night –'

At night? Fin sat up. 'What? . . . *Who?*'

Emily shook her head. 'I don't know who she is.'

'She?' The cold feeling she'd got earlier crept through Fin's body. 'A woman?'

Emily's face was quite wild. 'Yes! A horrible woman who smells of something rotten. She sits on the edge of my bed and makes me tell her things.'

'What things?'

Emily shook her head. 'I don't know.' She let her face fall into her hands. 'Oh, what must you think of me? You won't tell anyone, will you? Doctor Hunt says I should keep quiet, or people will say I'm mad and I'll be sent to an asylum.'

'He shouldn't say things like that to you!' Fin was tempted to say more, but she could see that Emily was already terrified, so she bit back her anger.

'Look, maybe you should tell Lady Worth about these dreams.'

Emily glanced up. 'I already have, lots of times. Mama says it's the illness, that I'm imagining things.'

Fin prised her hand from Emily's grasp – there were red marks on her palm from Emily's fingernails where she'd been gripping it so tightly. 'Listen,' Fin said. 'Why don't I keep you company tonight? I'll sleep on the couch over there.'

Emily shook her head. 'Doctor Hunt would never allow it. I asked before if Molly could stay with me, but he said it was detrimental to my health.'

'Well,' Fin said, 'I'll sneak down after everyone's gone to bed. That way, Doctor Hunt will be none the wiser, and no harm done.'

Emily broke into a grateful smile. 'Oh, would you, Fin?' she said. 'That would make me feel so much better.'

'Course I will. See you later then.'

Fin left her and went back to her own room. She spent the rest of the afternoon turning over the worrying things that Emily had told her. Eryk's stories had spooked her, but it was more than that. Fin had started to get the creeping feeling that something was very wrong. It was as if Castle Kaminski's strict rules and orderly perfection were a carefully constructed façade, and behind it all lurked something malevolent.

Fin didn't believe in ghouls and the undead, but there was one obvious villain who was very much alive. Dr Hunt. Fin didn't trust him an inch, and it wasn't just the callous things he said. For one, why did he insist on bleeding Emily every day? Fin didn't need to be a doctor to see there was hardly any blood left in her.

She wondered if she should say something to her aunt, but Emily had said she'd already spoken to her, and her worries had been dismissed. Fin had seen for herself the way Lady Worth fawned over the doctor, and if her own daughter couldn't persuade her, then Fin didn't stand a chance.

At dinner time, Mrs Benton came up to Fin's room to fetch her.

The last thing Fin needed was another humiliating session wrestling with the cutlery. 'Can't I have my supper up here?' she asked.

Mrs Benton shook her head. 'No, you can't. Madam says in this house we eat at the dining table or not at all.'

Fin crossed her arms. 'I'll have to go hungry then. Won't be the first time.'

Mrs Benton tutted. 'Eating your meals at the table is for your own good and Madam is only trying to help. Is it really too much to expect you to learn some manners, to learn to be a lady?'

Fin sighed. 'All right, I'll try . . . only not tonight. I can't face it.' She had no intention of trying, but at that moment she would have said anything to stop Mrs Benton going on.

The housekeeper tutted again and left without saying another word. But later, Molly appeared with bread and cheese and a cup of hot milk, saying Mrs Benton had sent it up.

When she'd eaten, Fin sat in the armchair by the window with Small on her lap. Her bedroom was at the back of the house, and she had a view across the garden to the marshes and the birch forest beyond. She watched as darkness fell and the moon climbed into the sky. Its ghostly face shone on the waters and silvered the rising mist.

Now that it was night she felt more than a little nervous. She desperately wanted to believe that Eryk had been making the whole story about the *strzyga* up, but she couldn't stop her mind from returning to the horror of the 'undead' Countess who fed on the memories of her own descendants.

'Thing is,' she said to Small, 'Emily didn't even remember Penelope, her *sister*.'

Small let out a sharp warning bark, but Fin shook her head determinedly. 'It can't be what Eryk said, Small. It must be Emily's illness what makes her confused.

There ain't no "undead Countess" – it's that doctor what's the problem. I can't let Eryk scare me with his horrible stories. There ain't no such thing as demons and ghouls.'

But for all her words, Fin still felt anxious, and from the way Small whined and growled at the rising moon, she knew he wasn't happy either.

When everyone had gone to bed and the house was quiet, Fin got up from the chair. Small had been snoozing, but as soon as she moved he was alert again. He jumped down and shook himself with a whine.

'Shh. Go back to sleep,' Fin said. 'Won't be long.'

Small ran ahead, getting himself between Fin and the door. 'Oh, Small! I know you don't want me to go,' she said. 'Only I promised.' She went past him, but he followed her. 'No, Small. You can't come. You're too noisy, and there'll be hell to pay if Lady Worth or that doctor finds out there's been a dog in the sickroom.'

She scooped him up and put him back on the armchair, where he curled up reluctantly and laid his head on his paws with an irritable huff. 'Good boy. Now stay.'

Fin crept out of her bedroom and along the corridor to the top of the staircase. There she waited, listening. Except for the monotonous tick of the grandfather clock in the hall, the house was silent. She tiptoed down the stairs to Emily's room and slipped inside. The curtains were half drawn and the room was flooded with moonlight.

She went to Emily's bedside. On the nightstand there was a glass with a residue of green syrup at the bottom. Fin picked it up and held it to her nose. It gave off a strong medicinal smell and Fin guessed it was a sleeping draught. Judging by her cousin's deep sleep, it was clearly working. She glanced around, but nothing drew her eye or looked out of place. The only sound was her cousin's soft breathing.

Fin felt a stab of anger towards Eryk. There was nothing going on here. True, she'd come partly to reassure Emily, but if it hadn't been for Eryk and his stories about the undead feeding at night, she wouldn't be in Emily's room at all. She'd let him wind her up good and proper and, tomorrow, she'd have to put up with him laughing at her. And what if someone came in and found her there? How would she explain it to them? She was in enough trouble as it was.

Fin went to the door, meaning to go back up to bed, but at that moment she heard footsteps approaching along the corridor. She looked around for somewhere to hide, and in a panic scooted under Emily's bed.

A moment later, she heard the door open and felt a rush of air, which carried a faint unpleasant smell, like the fish heads from Billingsgate Market that lay rotting on the banks of the Thames at low tide.

The counterpane covering the bed hung down to a few inches above the floorboards, giving Fin a view of the doctor's polished shoes as he crossed the room. Her heart hammered in her chest. What was *he* doing here?

But Dr Hunt was not alone. The moonlight shone on the hem of a shimmering black dress that slid across the floor, stopping next to the doctor's shoes, where it pooled on the oak boards like spilled ink.

'She is paler than last time.'

Fin froze at the sound of the unknown voice. It was a woman's, with a strong Polish accent, like Eryk's.

'You have been taking her blood for yourself, haven't you?' Her voice was hardly more than a jagged croak, as if forced from a throat full of broken glass.

'I had only a little of it.' Dr Hunt's tone, usually so superior, was now oily and grovelling. 'I was so hungry, mistress, I –'

His words were suddenly cut short. The doctor's heels pitched forward, as if he was standing on tiptoes, then his feet lifted clear of the floorboards altogether, and jerked this way and that in mid-air. Fin could not see exactly what was happening, but she could hear the sound of choking, and cold terror filled in the rest of the scene. Whoever this woman was, she had the strength to lift the doctor clean off his feet, and in her mind's eye Fin imagined the fist that must be tightening round the doctor's throat.

'She is mine!' the woman said. 'Find your blood elsewhere!'

She must have let him go then, because there was a heavy thud and the doctor fell to his knees and toppled forward, gasping, his forehead pressed against the floorboards at the woman's feet.

'If you let her die,' she said, 'like that other one . . .'

Fin's mouth went dry; 'the other one' must be Emily's dead sister Penelope.

'Forgive me, Countess,' the doctor croaked. 'Forgive me.'

Countess? Fin pressed a hand to her speeding heart. The demon that Eryk had conjured in the attic had come to life and was now stalking back and forth across the floorboards, no more than a few inches from where she lay hidden.

Fin heard the swish of her dress as the Countess moved to the head of Emily's bed. Her footsteps made no sound, and when the hem of her dress lifted a little, Fin saw her shoeless foot, with its peeling skin and yellow nails that curved beneath the toes like claws.

'They must all live,' the Countess said. 'At least until they have children of their own. But tell me more about the new child. She is six-fingered and red-haired, I am told.'

Fin's heart seemed to leap into her throat. The Countess meant *her*!

The doctor lifted his forehead from the floor but remained on his knees. 'Oh yes, mistress, an excellent specimen. Like the boy, she's somewhat different. She'll bring variety to your nourishment.'

'Different? In what way?'

The doctor shuffled forward on his knees. 'Why, her experiences! She has been living in poverty all this time. Imagine the taste of her memories! All that remembered misery, all that hunger and cold.'

The Countess's reply was dismissive. 'I do not thrive on half-forgotten misery or half-remembered joy. It is the *clarity* of the recollection that nourishes me. It is *intensity* I crave . . . Still, when I have finished here I will see her for myself.'

The bed springs above Fin's head sagged as the Countess settled herself on the edge of the mattress. 'Leave me now. I must feed.'

'Yes, mistress.' The doctor got to his feet and backed out of the room.

As soon as the door had closed behind him, the Countess began to whisper to Emily. 'Tell me a story. Speak, child, speak.'

Fin squeezed her eyes shut. If only she'd listened to Eryk, if only she'd asked what to do if she should ever meet a *strzyga*! She thought back to the stories she had heard as a small child. Maybe if she had a crucifix or a Bible or some other relic said to banish demons, she'd be able to do something to help, but what could she really do, unarmed, against a creature that could lift a man from his feet? She curled herself into a ball and covered her ears. There was nothing she could do, and she didn't want to know what happened next. She was thankful, therefore, when a timely piece of Ma Stump wisdom popped into her head: *Keep yer head down and look after yerself, cos no one else will.* For a few seconds, she was comforted by it. There was no need to do anything reckless. All she needed to do was stay quiet and hidden and wait for whatever was going on above her to be over.

But then Fin's eyes jumped open. No. Ma was wrong. Fin knew how it felt to be abandoned. What was she worth if she cowered here, keeping her head down and doing nothing? Emily had been kind to her, and she was a relative, her cousin. Like it or not, Fin was part of this strange family now, and if she had nothing to defend herself with, Emily had even less.

She clenched her fists, gathering her courage, then rolled away from where the Countess sat above her, emerging on the other side of the bed. She jumped up and grabbed the nearest thing to hand – a lamp – and swung it over her shoulder, ready to strike. 'Get off 'er!'

The Countess was taken by surprise. She had been leaning over Emily, coaxing her to speak, and for a second the scene seemed frozen in the moonlight, as if caught on a photographer's glass plate. The next moment, Emily's eyelids flickered and she woke from her drug-induced slumber. She raised her head and looked around, blinking sleepily at Fin and then at the woman sitting on her bed. 'Wh-who are you?' she stammered.

Her trembling question seemed to break the spell. The Countess pressed her palm to Emily's forehead and pushed her down. Then she stood and turned round.

Fin had thought the Countess's voice had sounded old, but her face, while not quite young, was somehow ageless. Her skin was smooth, as if it had been stretched taut and pinned across her bones, while the stink of her gave a hint of flesh rotting underneath. She had fiery eyes that reflected the silvery moonlight like a cat's, and Fin could feel the heat of the *strzyga*'s gaze. It burned her skin as it travelled from her six-fingered hand to her neck, her face, her hair.

The Countess opened her mouth wide. 'So it *is* you! The girl whose head is on fire!'

It was as if the demon already knew her, although Fin would not have forgotten if they had ever met before. She had no fangs, yet Fin could see two rows of teeth, one set hidden behind the other, laid flat against the roof of her dark mouth. Her triumphant voice flowed from this gaping maw, but it was not only words that spewed forth. The sounds she made transformed themselves into flesh, each taking on the shape of a hellish creature that seemed to be made from darkness.

More of them crept from the Countess's throat. Some were furred, some feathered, and all had round yellow eyes. They fell on to the counterpane and crawled or writhed or dragged themselves across the bed then tumbled to the ground, a waterfall of horror.

As they touched the floor, the creatures grew in size. Some surrounded Fin while others threw themselves upon her, clasping her tight with their clawed wings and feet. Fin's grip weakened on the lamp and her arm fell to her side. She longed to run, but the creatures seemed to have sucked the strength from her. She could not move.

Now the Countess approached, bringing the sickening stink of rot with her. 'Tell me! Speak!'

Her voice pierced Fin's mind, burrowed inside her head.

Immediately, she began to speak.

She didn't know what she said, but she felt something tearing in her mind and sensed a precious thing was being wrenched away. As she spoke, her words too took form, and a golden thread emerged from her mouth. The Countess's eyes glowed. She took hold of the thread and teased it out, winding it round and round her fingers.

Suddenly the door flew open, making the Countess turn abruptly. Small ran in, Eryk close behind. He held a bottle in his hand and he flung its contents into the Countess's face.

Her hands flew up and she staggered and turned about. Fin caught sight of her ruined face, the flesh steaming and eaten away as if Eryk's bottle had been full of caustic. The demon screamed out and her cry was answered, echoed by the furious howls of the creatures that had emerged from her throat. They left Fin and ran to her, climbing over each other in their desperation to return. But not all of them had managed to crawl back before the Countess began to change. Her form melted away, fading until she was made of nothing but a foggy mist. The fog drew itself together, and with a high-pitched sound like fingernails on glass, it flowed out of a crack in the window.

Now that their mistress was gone, the wails of the creatures left behind grew weak and pleading. Eryk stamped on one, leaving a sooty smudge on the floorboards. Fin followed suit, squashing the fleeing creatures beneath her feet. One scampered under the bed but Small dragged it out and shook it to pieces.

For a moment, they all stood still, breathing hard. Then Fin scooped Small into her arms and rushed to Emily's bedside. She was fast asleep, as if nothing at all had happened.

13

'I think she's all right,' Fin said.

'And you? I saw golden thread wrapped round Countess's fingers.'

'I don't know what I told her.' Fin put a hand to her throat. 'It's horrible to think she's stolen a piece of me. I don't even know which memory she took!'

'You will find out when you try to remember and memory is gone.'

'Did she ever steal any of yours?'

'No.'

Fin peered at Eryk in the gloom. 'How come? You've been at Castle Kaminski for months.'

'As soon as I come here, I suspect something wrong, but I do not know what. As precaution, each night I lock bedroom door and stuff keyhole and cracks in windows with rags I soak in mandrake root.'

'How'd you know to do that?'

'I learn to do as boy. In Poland, everyone in Kaminski family is taught.'

Fin shivered and slumped down on the end of Emily's bed. It was clearly a dangerous thing to be a member of the Kaminski clan. 'What were them . . . them *things* that came out of her?' she said.

'They were her courtiers from when she lived, hundreds of years ago. Now they are her familiars.'

Fin winced. Everything Eryk had told her in the attic was true. 'Listen . . .' she began, 'I'm sorry I didn't believe you before. I thought you was winding me up.'

Fin was expecting a 'told you so' from Eryk, but he only nodded solemnly. 'Is not your fault. You did not grow up in my village, or you would know about *strzygi*.'

Fin smiled at him. 'If it hadn't been for you, I would've been done for. How did you know to come?'

'Small. He is good dog. He scratch my door and bring me here.'

'Course he did. He always knows when something's up.' Fin squeezed Small a little too enthusiastically and he let out an indignant yelp.

There was a darkness in Eryk's voice when he continued: 'Then I see Doctor Hunt.'

'He's on *her* side,' Fin said. 'He's been taking Emily's blood, feeding off her.'

Eryk nodded. 'I never like him, but I did not know he is familiar . . . then I see him leaving Emily's room. I do not have to guess what happen, so I fetch bottle I bring from Poland.'

'What *was* that stuff you chucked in the Countess's face?'

'Is made from root of mandrakes growing on grave of our ancestors.'

'Will it kill her?'

'No. It hurt her, but she will soon get better.'

'Oh . . . Got any more of it?'

'No. Is from Poland.'

'Oh.' Fin hung her head. 'So what'll we do? From what those two were saying, we're next.'

Eryk sat down beside her. 'What they say?'

'The doctor said we would add "variety" to the Countess's diet.' She shivered at the thought, remembering how the Countess had turned her hungry gaze on her, the strange words she had spoken. 'It was almost as if she *knew* me.'

Eryk swallowed. 'What?'

'I don't know what she meant, but she said I was the girl whose head is on fire —'

Eryk jumped up. 'I knew it! I say this first time I see you! Remember? And Lady Worth is angry with me?' He began to pace back and forth, speaking to himself in Polish.

'What? What is it?' Fin said.

Eryk turned to her excitedly. 'Is written in *History of the Kaminskis*, the only one who can break the family curse is girl with head on fire.' He pointed to Fin. 'And your hair is red, like fire.'

Fin shifted uncomfortably. 'Lots of people have red hair.'

Eryk raised an eyebrow. 'Not in Kaminski family, and anyway, Countess say it. She *know*.'

'But . . . but I'm not even a proper Kaminski!'

Eryk sat down next to her. 'You are girl with head on fire. You must accept.'

Fin turned away from him. It was the last thing she wanted to hear. The thought of being connected to that terrifying demon, of being in any way involved in this unfolding nightmare was too much to bear. Yet here was Eryk, telling her she had more than a bit part – she was right in the middle of it all, the person who, despite never having heard of *strzygi* before that day, was supposed to somehow sort it all out.

For a while, the two of them sat in silence, lost in their own thoughts. Then Fin raised her head. She was frightened, but, as before, she knew she must put aside her own fear and think of Emily. 'We got to get that doctor out this house,' she said.

'How?'

'We have to tell Lady Worth what's going on.'

Eryk sighed. 'I hope she will believe . . . She thinks is all superstition. And she has *big* trust for Doctor Hunt.'

Fin's loathing for the man welled up, as bitter as bile. 'He's the one what killed Penelope.'

'How you know this?'

'The Countess was angry with the doctor about it; she said we must all live and have children of our own.'

'This make sense. If no more children in Kaminski family, *strzyga* will starve.'

Fin got up. 'Come on, let's wake Lady Worth. None of us is safe until that blood-sucking familiar is out of this house. She'll *have* to believe us when we tell her what we've seen.'

Fin and Eryk went upstairs to Lady Worth's room with Small trotting along behind. They knocked loudly, and after a minute she came to the door, pulling on a dressing gown.

Lady Worth did not look pleased to see them. 'What on earth is the meaning of this?' she demanded. 'It's the middle of the night.'

'Can we come in?' Fin said. 'We've got to tell you something.'

She looked from Fin to Eryk and narrowed her eyes. 'Eryk? This had better not be another one of your ridiculous stories.'

'No,' Fin said. 'I promise it ain't.'

Reluctantly, Lady Worth stood back from the door and motioned for them to enter. Once they were inside she folded her arms. 'Well, what is it that's so important that it couldn't possibly wait until a decent hour?'

'It's about Emily,' Fin began.

'What about her? Is she all right?' She made to go to the door.

'She's fine now, but . . .' Fin glanced at Eryk. It was difficult to know exactly what to say that would convince Lady Worth. 'What Eryk told you before, it's true. I didn't believe him at first neither, but *strzygi* really do exist and there's this one called the Countess, who's our ancestor, and she came here tonight to steal Emily's memories – which is what keeps her alive, even though she's really old and ought to be dead by now – and Doctor Hunt –' At the mention of the doctor's name Small growled deep in his throat. 'Well,' Fin continued, 'he's helping her and he's taking Emily's blood and –'

Lady Worth held up a hand. '*Enough!*' She turned on Eryk. 'This is your doing! You've infected the girl with your superstitious bunkum. I fail to understand how you could come up here in the middle of the night and try to frighten me with your falsehoods . . . My poor daughter is gravely ill, yet you seek to besmirch the reputation of Doctor Hunt, the only person who can help her, the man who has moved heaven and earth to make her well again!' She shook her head in disbelief. 'Never have I seen such a lack of gratitude as I see in you two. I took you in when you had nowhere to go, and yet you repay me with these wicked lies!'

Eryk looked at her sadly. 'Is not lies,' he said quietly. 'Doctor Hunt is Countess's familiar. Emily will not get better while he is in this house.'

'Erik's right,' Fin said urgently. 'You have to believe us. I saw him, tonight, with the Countess, in Emily's room –'

Lady Worth turned on Fin. 'You were in my daughter's bedroom?'

'I . . . I was worried about her. She was afraid. She said someone came at night and after what Eryk said about the *strzyga* –'

'Yes, I see now. *After what Eryk said*, was it? Neither of you care about the damage you do. Neither of you have any idea what the doctor has done for this family. He has worked tirelessly, helping me when there was no one else to turn to –' She put a hand to her forehead and let out a sob.

'I'm sorry,' Fin said, 'but Doctor Hunt ain't what he seems. And it's worse than that. He's the one what killed Penelope! You've got to get rid of him before he does the same to Emily!'

Lady Worth had been drying her eyes on the sleeve of her dressing gown, but on hearing this she stopped. 'Penelope?' For a moment she looked confused, but then her face hardened. 'This is outrageous! How dare you suggest that Doctor Hunt had anything to do with that tragedy!' She got hold of Fin's arm and marched her out into the corridor. 'We will go and see the doctor now and find out what he has to say about all this!'

Fin wrenched her arm away. 'I ain't going anywhere near that monster. He's a parasite, a murderer. It's him what's made Emily so weak and pale.'

Lady Worth put her hands over her ears. 'Stop it! I'm not listening to any more of this.' She turned and hurried away down the stairs, towards Dr Hunt's quarters.

'She'll tell him what we said!' Fin grabbed Eryk's hand and pulled him after her. 'We got to get out of here!'

Fin and Eryk, with Small close behind, started down the staircase, but there was an angry shout from below – 'Where are they?' It was the doctor.

From the top floor came the sound of doors opening and raised voices as the servants, woken by the commotion, came out to see what the matter was. 'We'll be caught in the middle,' Fin said in a panic, scooping up Small and hugging him close. 'Come on – this way.'

They ran back up the stairs and along the corridor to the plain back staircase that Mrs Benton had led Fin up when she'd first arrived. It was deserted, and they raced down and reached the kitchen without meeting anyone. From there, they ran to the boot room and pulled on hats and coats before slipping out into the night. Behind them, a great hubbub came from the floors above. Someone had been sent to fetch Fin and Eryk from their rooms, and now the search was spreading out across the house.

14

'Quick,' Fin said. 'It won't take 'em long to realize we've run.'

They sprinted across the lawn and tumbled down the steep bank of the moat. Although it had been drained long ago, a thick layer of stinking mud on the bottom sucked at Fin's boots. It was harder to get up the other side. Fin lifted Small up first, then clasped her hands together and gave Eryk a leg up. When he'd scrambled on to the bank, he put out a hand and pulled her up after him. They dashed along the paths between the flower beds on the other side of the moat, and had just reached the cover of the hedgerow when the back door opened again.

Light spilled out and three figures emerged. 'Fetch my horse!' Dr Hunt commanded, and the other two figures took off towards the stables. When they had gone, the doctor peered into the night. Raising his head, he sniffed at the air.

Fin shrank back into the hedgerow. 'What's he doing?'

'A familiar is special. He can smell like dog,' Eryk said.

Fin held her breath as the doctor advanced across the lawn, still sniffing at the air. He'd reached the edge of the moat, and was within sixty feet of them, when the two footmen returned with his horse. The doctor continued to peer into the darkness, his gaze raking over the flower beds to the hedgerow where they were hidden. Then he turned and went back to the house. There, he mounted his waiting steed and galloped off round the side of the house towards the road.

Fin breathed a sigh of relief. She was shaking and weak from the fright. 'What'll we do now? We can't go back.'

'You are right,' Eryk said. 'We have nothing to protect us from familiar. We must run away fast. He will soon know we are not on road.'

They crawled through a gap in the hedge and scrambled to their feet. Clouds covered the moon and it was pitch-dark, but Fin remembered the view from the top floor of the house, the dark line of the birch forest in the distance. There, the trees grew too close together for a rider on a horse to get through. If they could make it that far, they'd be safe. But first they'd have to cross the miles of marshy land that led away from the back of the garden, a terrain dotted with ponds, flat and devoid of cover but for the reeds and the odd hummock of gorse and hawthorn.

Fin couldn't see the paths that wound between the bogs, but just as he used to do on Hackney Marsh at night, Small began to sniff them out. In the little light there was, Fin could just make out his white fur, darting ahead.

As she ran, Fin stumbled on a root and, putting out her hand to save herself, caught it in something thorny.

Eryk helped her up. 'You are hurt?'

Her hand was stinging, and she realized the thorns had broken the skin. 'It's nothing,' she said.

'Is bleeding?'

She sucked her fingers and tasted metal. 'Only a bit.'

Fin heard the sound of tearing and Eryk took her hand and wrapped something tightly round it.

'What's that?' she asked.

'My shirt. Must cover wound. Doctor can smell human blood.'

When he'd bandaged her hand, they hurried on.

'At least the doctor won't be able to see us,' Fin said.

Eryk made a non-committal sound in his throat.

'What's that mean?' Fin said. 'Familiars can see in the dark now, can they?'

'Yes,' he replied, and Fin could hear the unease in Eryk's voice. 'Familiar can see in dark. Like owl.'

They'd been running across the marshes for at least an hour when a horse whinnied nearby. They crouched down among the long grass and Fin drew her coat round Small, so his bright fur would not give them away. Now they were still, they could hear the to-and-fro call of night birds and, not far behind, the doctor's low voice, encouraging his horse as it picked its way across the marsh. Fin licked a finger and held it up. The breeze was coming from behind them, and she hoped this meant the doctor would not be able to sniff them out. But somehow he must have sensed they were close, because the doctor fell silent. Now the only sounds were the clink of the horse's bridle, which seemed very near.

Fin lay still, listening out for the horse. From time to time it snorted or its bridle jingled. And now, to Fin's relief, each time she heard it, the horse seemed a little further off. Even so, she felt for Eryk's hand. She dared not make a sound and her senses felt stretched as she listened, trying to gauge the horse's position, starting at every rustle in the undergrowth. She couldn't see anything in the darkness, but if Eryk was right, the doctor could. They were helpless as mice, caught against the ground, not knowing from which direction the predator would strike.

Suddenly, the clouds above them broke and the edge of the moon shone through. For a second, a swathe of marshy land was illuminated by silvery light, before the clouds drew themselves back together and plunged them into darkness once more. But in that brief moment of moonlight, a horrifying scene had flashed before Fin's eyes. She saw the doctor crawling across the ground towards them, his cloak spread out around him like the black wings of a giant bat.

He had tricked them. Realizing they would be listening for the horse, he had dismounted and left it some way off, while he himself crept silently towards them.

They jumped up and ran.

'Split up!' Fin cried. 'He can't chase us all down.'

Eryk peeled away to her left and Small to her right. Now, she had to find her way without the beacon of Small's white body leading her. But although the moon had only lit the scene for a second, Fin's memory had mapped the route between the bogs, the way to the edge of the forest beyond. She stopped to catch her breath and stood, listening for the sounds of pursuit. The gallop of hooves sounded nearby, but the drumming seemed to be coming from ahead of her, not behind.

Again the clouds parted and Fin glimpsed the edge of the forest, not more than a hundred feet away. But between her and the treeline was a wide stretch of boggy ground with only a narrow pathway across, and on the other side of that was the doctor, remounted on his horse.

'Stay where you are,' he shouted, 'or I will run you down!' He urged his steed on to the path and began to make his way towards her.

Fin turned to get away, but what was the point? She was alone, and too tired to run any further. There was no cover, nowhere to hide. The only chance of escape was to reach the forest, but her route was blocked by the doctor and his steed. *Unless* . . . Fin didn't know much about horses, but she knew of many people who'd been crushed under the wheels of carriages . . . She hesitated, imagining the heavy hooves raining down on her, crushing her bones.

For a moment, she hung her head, too terrified to move. But then, glancing up, she saw the clouds roll away, leaving the shining moon and a clear sky dotted with thousands of bright stars. She was freezing, exhausted and more exposed than ever, yet she felt the silvery rays on her face like the warmth of the sun and her fear melted away.

Just then, Small appeared out of the gloom and ran to her side. He darted back and forth, barking and growling as the doctor and his horse approached. Fin was no longer alone, and Small's ferocity gave her courage. She gritted her teeth.

'Come on, Small! Let's rush 'im! *Charge!*'

Together they hurtled along the narrow pathway towards the doctor. The horse faltered at the sudden commotion, but the doctor dug in his heels. He urged the steed into a gallop. As it bore down on them, Fin stopped running and crouched in the middle of the narrow path.

There was no way round. Either the horse would stop or it would trample her.

She clutched Small to her side, and when the doctor was almost upon them she shouted, 'Now!' She leaped up, waving her arms above her head, shouting for all she was worth, while Small raced forward, barking and snapping.

The horse screamed and reared up, its hooves flailing at the air above Fin's head. It wheeled away to avoid her, tipping the doctor from the saddle and flinging him into the bog. The horse turned tail and galloped back along the path towards the forest.

The doctor lay face down, his body sunk in the mud up to his waist, one arm flung out across the path. He stayed completely still.

Was he unconscious? Dead?

Fin couldn't be certain. She scooped Small into her arms. 'Let's get out of here,' she said. She edged towards the doctor, keeping as far to the other side of the narrow path as she could and began to step round him.

Suddenly a hand shot out and grabbed Fin's ankle. She screamed as he pulled her over and she fell heavily on to the path. The doctor lifted his head and Fin saw his narrowed eyes, the moonlight glinting on his triumphant grin. Small leaped from her arms and tore at the doctor's fist, while Fin kicked at him with her other foot. But the doctor held on. He climbed hand over hand, gradually pulling himself out of the bog.

The doctor had managed to get to his knees and was half out of the mud when a harsh cry cut through the night. Fin turned her head to see Eryk hurtling down the path towards them. He was dragging a huge branch behind him, which he lifted high into the air, bringing it down on the familiar's skull with a sickening crack. The doctor cried out in pain and fury. He released Fin's ankle and fell back into the clutches of the bog.

'Come!' Eryk pulled Fin to her feet and the three of them ran along the path, away from the flailing arms and curses of the doctor, into the gloom of the forest.

They ran through the leafless trees until exhaustion forced them to stop and rest. Fin bent over double, resting her hands on her knees as she gasped for breath. 'Do you think he'll follow us?' she said.

Eryk nodded. 'Soon as he gets out of mud, he will come after us.'

Fin remembered what Eryk had said about the doctor's night vision that was as keen as an owl's, his sense of smell that was as sharp as a dog's.

Meanwhile, Small ran in circles, snuffing at the air, his growls and whines a message that they should waste no time.

'We must keep going,' Eryk said. 'Get far from castle.'

'But which way?'

They both looked up, through the bare branches of the trees to the starry sky above.

'There!' Eryk said. 'North star. This way.' He pointed into the darkness between the trees, and they set off.

The spike of shock and fear after the flight from the doctor had kept them going, but now they were bone-tired, hungry and thirsty. When they came to a stream, Fin and Eryk lay down on the bank, scooped the water up in their hands and gulped it down.

When they had quenched their thirst Eryk said, 'Let us walk in river. Will hide our smell.'

They took off their boots and stockings and walked through the ankle-deep water, Fin carrying Small in her arms. The stream ran through the trees, north to south, and took them out of their way, but it would be worth it if it threw the doctor off their scent. A mile downstream, the water got too deep for them to carry on and they climbed out on the other side, shivering with the cold. When they'd rubbed the blood back into their feet and pulled their boots back on, they took off again, using the stars as their guides.

Most of the time, Fin stumbled on, her thoughts taken up with the darkness that surrounded her, the many hazards beneath her feet. But every now and then the evening's events would flash into her mind – her flawless memory perfectly recreating the tearing feeling as the Countess pulled on the golden thread that had emerged from her mouth, winding it round and round her fingers. The image filled her with fear, and she found herself half wishing she had the foggier mind of other people.

At last they came to the edge of the birch forest, and a fresh piece of marshland stretched out before them. Faraway on the other side, Fin could see a new line of trees, which must, she thought, be the great Epping Forest. Beyond that lay London, the place she knew so well it was like it was a part of her. They were far from the northern road or any dwelling here, in true wilderness, and Fin gratefully breathed in the familiar smell of the marshes.

Unlike Fin, Eryk was not comforted by the new vista. He grabbed her arm. 'Look!' He pointed towards a distant light in the darkness. 'And over there!' He pulled her round to look in the opposite direction, where more pinpricks of light flickered in the gloom. 'They are coming for us,' he said. 'We must turn back, hide in forest.'

But Fin had seen lights out on the marshes at night many times before. 'It's nothin' to be scared of,' she said. 'Only will-o'-the-wisps.'

'What is this?'

'In the olden days, people used to say will-o'-the-wisps were demons and ghosts what lure travellers to their deaths in the quicksands –' Eryk's grip on Fin's arm grew tighter and she realized her explanation was only making things worse. 'Course,' she said, changing tack, 'now we knows it's only marsh fire, humours what bubble out of the bogs and catch light. No one believes in ghosts no more.'

Eryk released her arm, but he was not completely mollified. 'There is *strzyga*,' he muttered to himself, 'so why not ghost?'

A bitter wind had got up, and now that they were not on the move and had lost the cover of the trees, they all began to shiver with the cold.

'Well, there's one good thing,' Fin said. 'With all the lights from them will-o'-the-wisps out there, we can have a blaze of our own and no one'll be any the wiser.'

They collected armfuls of firewood from the edge of the forest and struck out across the marsh. Small found a dry, raised patch of ground surrounded by gorse bushes, announcing with several huffs that it was a good place to stop and rest.

Eryk piled up dry grass along with the firewood they'd collected, while Fin took out her mother's brass tinderbox and set about getting a spark to catch a piece of the scorched linen packed inside. With the help of the wind, they soon had a blaze going and they huddled close, holding their freezing hands out to the flames.

'I can't stop thinking about Emily,' Fin said. 'We shouldn't ha' left her behind. She'll be at the mercy of the Countess and that doctor, and no one to help her.'

Eryk winced. 'I scared about her too,' he admitted, 'but what else can we do? The only way to help her is to break curse and destroy *strzyga*.'

'How?'

'I do not know.' He glanced at her and narrowed his eyes. 'But maybe you do. You are Magdalena Kaminski, girl with head on fire.'

'You keep saying that,' Fin snapped. 'But I *ain't* her.'

'Who then?'

'I'm Fin, and more than half of me was made by living in Ma's attic, and leeching on the marshes, and fighting with Snot and George.'

'Yes, but other half is in your blood.' He leaned towards her. 'You are just like typical Kaminski.'

'How d'you make that out?'

'What you do tonight. You stand up to doctor. You are brave, like all our ancestors.'

'Don't be stupid. I was bloomin' terrified! Thought my head was gonna get stoved in by them hooves.'

'Yes, you face death and terror. This exactly what brave is. You must accept truth, that you are Magdalena

Kaminski.' He held out his hand, and linked his extra finger to Fin's, like in the family crest. '*Lojalność.*'

'What does that mean?'

'It mean "loyalty". Is special Kaminski family greeting. You must learn, now you are one of us.'

Fin suddenly found tears springing to her eyes and she turned away. What was she crying for? Many times, she'd been told she was useless and unwanted, and had always stayed dry-eyed, but now this boy she hardly knew said one kind word, told her she belonged, and she started blubbing like a baby? She quickly wiped her tears on her sleeve and hoped he hadn't noticed.

Eryk must have realized, though, because when she turned back he was staring studiously into the fire. 'We need plan,' he said. 'I have been thinking. There are stories in *History of the Kaminskis*. I look for it in attic but don't find, so I ask Mrs Benton. She say it has been taken.'

'By who?'

'By Bashka.'

'Aunty Bashka, the actress?'

'Yes. So, we must find her and the book. She will help us.'

'Have you met her?'

Eryk shook his head.

'What makes you think she'll help us, then?'

'She is Kaminski,' Eryk said, looking affronted. 'Is duty. Of course she will help. Every Kaminski take oath, as child, to help other Kaminskis and destroy the *strzyga*.'

Fin thought back to the picture they'd seen in the attic at the castle, the three sisters in their flowery head-dresses. More than likely, this aunt would turn out to be a younger version of Lady Worth. Fin was sick of the dutiful charity of the Kaminskis, and even more sick of having to be grateful for it. She was glad to be away from the oppressive rules of Castle Kaminski and reluctant at the prospect of being judged by another one of the Kaminski sisters.

'We don't even know where she lives,' she said. 'Anyways, we don't need her help. I'm more than used to looking out for meself, me an' Small –'

'We must find book,' Eryk said, cutting her off. 'And we need family help. We cannot do this alone. You do not know what Countess is like.'

Fin folded her arms. 'I just met her, *and* I lost a memory, so I reckon I know what she's like well enough.'

Eryk turned towards her. 'Kaminski family have known Countess for hundreds of years. We are food to her, and she destroy the minds of our ancestors so she can live. Now she know you are girl with head on fire, she will send out all her familiars.'

'Why? What's so special about this "girl with her head on fire" then?'

'I do not remember everything, but is in book, and every Kaminski child is told story of this girl. She is only one who can break curse and destroy Countess – but she is also only one who can make Countess young again and live forever.'

The wind tore at Eryk's dark hair and there were shadows beneath his eyes and in the hollows of his face. 'You are life or death to her. She will not stop until she find you.'

16

At dawn, a ribbon of velvety pink mist lay across the horizon. The fire had burned down to embers and Fin was stiff with cold. She sat up and rubbed the blood back into her limbs. She'd been woken by the honking of swans, and she watched as the flock descended on to a wide stretch of water. They crash-landed, feet stretched out in front of them, wings flapping clumsily at the air. But once down, they curved their necks gracefully and ruffled their white feathers as if they were made of icing sugar and had just alighted on a frosted cake.

Eryk was snoring quietly, and she gave him a shove. 'Wake up.'

He let out a pitiful moan. 'I am hungry.'

'Me too.' Fin glanced around. 'I'll catch us an eel.' She got up and tried to break off one of the dry rushes that surrounded them, but it was as tough as rope. 'If I had a knife, I could cut these and make a trap.'

Eryk had been watching, bemused, but now he smiled and pulled a penknife from his pocket. He took over the reed-cutting while Fin wove them together. She made a narrow ring and attached long lengths of reed all the way round, tying them together at the bottom until she had made a long, thin basket. 'Now we need some bait,' she told him.

They dug around the roots of the reeds until they found some worms and Fin put them in the bottom of her trap. She scouted the area and found a shallow stream, where she laid the trap with the open end facing upstream. 'Now we wait.'

Eryk's stomach growled noisily. 'How long?'

Fin tapped her nose. 'Them eels will soon sniff out the bait.'

True enough, after they'd waited a while, Fin checked the trap and found two small eels inside. She gutted and skewered each one on a sharpened length of reed, cooked them over the embers of last night's fire, and shared them out between the three of them.

By the time they'd finished eating, the sun had risen above the reed beds. The wide sky was pale blue and cloudless as they began the journey towards Epping Forest and, beyond that, London. After the terror of the night before, Fin felt buoyant. It was going to be a fine day, and she didn't even mind the idea of finding this Aunty Bashka, so long as she was back on home turf.

As they walked along, Eryk asked Fin how she had learned to catch eels.

'Been doing it for years,' she replied. 'Ma sometimes had one too many, and thought she were back in the boxing ring again –'

Eryk looked horrified. 'She hit you?'

Fin shrugged. 'Only if you didn't move quick enough. Anyways, when Ma were on the rum, it were best to stay out her way, and me and Snot and George used to camp out on the marshes. That's when I learned to catch eels for supper. It were Snot's favourite.'

Eryk was not convinced by her cheerful tone. 'This Ma does not sound like good person,' he said.

But Fin was still stuck in the habit of thinking the best of Ma. In the past, she'd had no choice but to make excuses for her. And now, despite all the evidence to the contrary, Fin still couldn't admit she was a wrong 'un. 'It weren't really her fault,' she said. 'It were the booze.'

They walked across the marshes, following the winding paths between streams and ponds, until the ground rose and dried out as they reached the edge of the forest. Once among the trees, they used the sun to guide them south and west.

By midday, they came to the other side of the forest and a river with a footbridge across. They quenched their thirst, then stopped to rest on the riverbank.

Fin glanced over at Eryk. He was covered in mud and had bits of dried leaf and twig stuck in his hair and burrs attached to his coat. Fin guessed she didn't look much better. She soaked her handkerchief in the river water. 'Better give ourselves a wash,' she said. 'We'll attract attention looking like this when we get to town.'

'Why?' Eryk said. 'I heard London is full with dirty children.'

'Yeah, but not many of 'em as is dressed in tweed and velvet.' She handed him the handkerchief. ''Ere, can you do my face?'

When Eryk had wiped the dirt from Fin's cheeks, she returned the favour and then they sponged the mud off their clothes as best they could. Small was filthy too, and although he tried to dodge her she managed to grab him and, ignoring his pitiful whining, wiped the worst of it off.

She stood back to take in the effect. 'Hmm,' she said, 'neither of you looks too bad now.'

'But I *feel* bad.' Eryk rubbed his stomach. 'I am hungry again.'

'You're always hungry,' Fin said, although to be fair, it was a long time since they'd eaten, and the eels had only been small. She pointed across the footbridge, to the houses in the distance. 'Come on! Not far to a pie shop now.'

Eryk still looked worried. 'We have no money,' he said. 'How will we buy?'

'I know a place where we can sell our clothes. It's only a couple of miles, and not too close to my usual stomping ground.'

They crossed the footbridge and emerged from the forest into the backstreets of Chingford. Fin soon found the main road that led south to Walthamstow, and along the way they came to a rag market where the poor got fourth-hand the things the rich had bought new.

Although the sun was shining, the drains were blocked after the recent rains and the market square was filled with a shallow lake of mud. The costermongers had set their stalls and barrows, mounded with potatoes and turnips and the frilly heads of cabbages, on the pavements round the edge, where it was drier. Meanwhile, their customers were forced to pick their way through the stinking sludge. The hawkers took advantage of the slow-moving crowd, shoving their baskets of apples and onions under the noses of

potential customers and shouting the prices in their faces, whether they liked it or not.

Before joining the throng, Fin scooped Small into her arms so he wouldn't get all muddy again. Eryk looked around, mouth open, entranced.

'I have never seen so many people,' he said. He watched a gang of dust women go past, carrying the spoils from the dust heap on their backs.

Fin gave him a nudge. 'Don't stare! We already stick out like two sore thumbs.'

But Eryk wasn't listening. 'Look!' he said, sloshing his way over to a stall offering calf's ears stuffed with forcemeat, and something called 'The Lord Mayor's Potage', which turned out to be a soup made of a pig's head.

Fin also kept her eyes peeled but, unlike Eryk, she was not captivated by the sights and sounds of the market; she'd seen it all before. Instead, she kept a lookout for the gangs of beggars and dippers who liked to work a crowded street. Even better if people were watching their step in the mud – they could be robbed all the more easily if they were busy looking down at their feet.

Sure enough, she soon spotted two ragged boys and a girl. They were watching the crowd, and as Fin and Eryk went by, the urchins signalled to another group of lurkers on the other side of the street.

Fin grabbed Eryk's arm. 'We been marked!' she hissed.

'What?' Eryk was completely unaware, too busy gawking at a monkey sitting on the shoulder of a man selling ballads and penny dreadfuls.

'We got to keep moving,' Fin said, hurrying him on. 'That gang of pickpockets back there, they've noticed us.'

'But we have no money –'

'It ain't only cash they steal. They'll have the clothes off our backs soon as –'

Just then, a thin girl with her hair in tangles bumped into Fin. She was sent staggering and almost dropped Small.

'Aw, now, miss. Terrible sorry,' the girl said loudly, while pretending to help Fin right herself. But Fin felt a tell-tale tug on her coat and spun round, just in time to see a tiny boy behind her pull his hand away and melt back into the crowd.

'Oy!' Fin yelled, and she turned back to give the girl what for, but now she'd disappeared too.

Fin clutched frantically at her coat. Luckily, she'd put the tinderbox in her inside pocket and the thieves hadn't got it. But Eryk hadn't been so lucky. When he checked his suit pockets he found them cut and his penknife gone.

'Everything all right here, miss?'

Fin and Eryk had been so busy, they hadn't seen the bobby approach. He was looking down at them, frowning, clearly wondering what two grubby but well-dressed children were doing by themselves in the middle of a rag market. 'Now then, what have we got here?' he said. 'Where are your parents, young 'uns?'

Small growled at the policeman, but Fin quietened him and put on her best voice and smile. 'Why, Officer, it's kind of you to ask. Papa was just here . . .' She pretended to look around. 'Oh, no need to worry – there he is!' She grabbed Eryk's hand and pulled him into the crowd.

'Why you don't tell him we are robbed?' Eryk said as she dragged him away.

Fin shook her head. 'Can't never trust a bluebottle . . . 'cept for one good 'un I know,' she said, thinking of Sergeant Malone. 'Anyways, he'd want names and addresses and all sorts. Before you know it, we'd be the ones accused of stealing.' She glanced down at her expensive velvet dress and then at Eryk's tweed jacket and trousers. 'It's this bloomin' finery what's causing all the problems. We need to get shot of these togs.'

17

They continued along the main road, leaving the chaos of the market behind, and soon reached Walthamstow. There, in a backstreet crammed with filthy tenements, was a broker's shop. A trestle table was set up outside, laden with shoes and boots, and hanging from pegs driven into the walls was displayed a multitude of shirts and dresses and petticoats. Everything for sale was second-hand, but some items looked hardly worn, while others were covered in stains and barely more than rags.

'Might look suspicious if we both try to sell our stuff,' she said. 'You stay here with Small, – and don't speak to no one.' She crossed over to the shop, leaving Eryk on the other side of the street.

Fin went up to the stout woman wearing a mob cap and apron who stood in the doorway. She held out the skirt of the midnight-blue velvet dress she was wearing.

'What will you give me for this?' she asked.

The woman sucked her teeth. 'We don't take stolen goods.'

Cheek of it, Fin thought, since everyone thereabouts knew half the woman's stock was knock-off. But it was hardly the time to get into a slanging match.

'Oh no,' Fin said, smiling sweetly, 'it ain't stolen. It were a gift.'

The woman smiled back. 'Well, if you say so,' and she pointed over her shoulder. 'Slip it off and I'll have a look.'

Fin selected a dress from the pegs that wasn't too badly stained and went inside. The clothes hanging outside covered the windows, cutting out the light, and the shop's interior was dim. Worn and mildewed items of furniture were stacked against the walls, and there were more trestle tables loaded with pots and pans, mangles and laundry tubs. Fin squeezed between the tables and went to the back of the shop, where a bed sheet had been pinned across a cupboard door to serve as a changing room. The cupboard was stuffed with brushes and brooms, and there was a bucket full of scummy water with a grubby sponge floating on top in case anyone was tempted to have a wash.

Fin took off the velvet dress and put on the one she'd taken from the peg. It smelled like everything else in the shop, a mixture of unwashed bodies, dirty water and mildew.

Fin went back out and handed her dress to the shopkeeper. The woman pursed her lips and held the gown up to the light. 'Hmmm, nice bit of material,' she said, 'but it's got dirt on it.'

'That'll brush off easy, once it's dry,' Fin replied.

The shopkeeper lifted the dress to her nose. 'Stinks a bit.'

'That'll soon go if you hang it in the fresh air.'

The woman held it against her body, as if she were thinking of wearing it herself. 'Well, all right then, I'll give you four shillings.'

'Come off it!' Fin said. 'That velvet is quality – just look at the colour.'

'Five then,' the woman said grudgingly, 'but that's my final offer.'

Fin haggled a while longer, managing to get six shillings as well as the dress she was wearing and a woollen cap thrown in to hide her long red hair. The shopkeeper spat on her palm and they shook on it. 'Come back when you wants to sell the rest,' she said, eyeing Fin's coat and boots.

Fin drew back. She was glad to get rid of the dress, but she'd never had her own coat and boots before. She'd have to be very hungry indeed before she parted with them.

She ran across the road to where Eryk and Small were waiting. 'Look,' she said, opening her hand. 'I got money!'

She led Eryk to another broker's shop, where they sold his tweed suit in exchange for another six shillings and a less fancy set of clothes.

'Now we've got twelve shillings,' Fin said. 'What d'you fancy to eat?'

Eryk closed his eyes. 'A very big bowl of bigos.'

'What's that?'

'Is Polish dish.'

'We don't get much of that round 'ere,' she said, 'but I know a decent pie and mash shop. That'll 'ave to do us instead.'

For sixpence, they bought three portions with green liquor sauce. They were so famished, Fin and Eryk ate theirs standing up, right outside the shop, while Small gobbled his out of a piece of newspaper on the pavement.

'Mmm. Fit for a queen,' Fin said, as she wolfed down the last morsel.

'Food of gods,' Eryk agreed. 'But now what we do?'

It was a good question. Evening was coming on and the lamp-lighters were already out. It would be dangerous to sleep out of doors, not to mention cold.

'They ain't pretty, but we could find a doss house for the night somewhere close by,' Fin said.

Eryk nodded. 'But first we look for Bashka.'

Fin sighed. 'I suppose there ain't no harm in going up the West End for an hour or two. We can ask around at the theatres, see if anyone knows her up there. But don't get yer hopes up. London ain't a village in the mountains. There's loads of theatres, not to mention the music halls and 'undreds of penny gaffs.'

It was quite a way from Walthamstow to the West End. They took a horse-drawn omnibus, and Fin hid Small under her coat since animals weren't allowed. They went up on the top deck, and Fin pointed out the various sights. As they travelled west, they passed Victoria Park and Eryk was shocked to see the homeless poor staking out a place to sleep under the trees. They trundled along Cheapside and past the great dome of St Paul's Cathedral, then down Ludgate Hill and Fleet

Street before the omnibus eventually stopped in Trafalgar Square, where they jumped off.

Eryk stared open-mouthed at the two great fountains, then up at Admiral Nelson standing on top of his towering column. The grand buildings that edged the square were in stark contrast to the slums of Walthamstow. 'Who live *here*?' he asked.

'Rich people and paintings,' Fin said, nodding towards the vast portico of the National Gallery.

They walked north, and in a couple of minutes came to Leicester Square, where the Alhambra stood. The music hall was huge, taking up the whole north side of the square.

'Is like Turkey,' Eryk said, marvelling at the impressive dome and the twin minarets that rose into the sky on either side.

A crowd was gathered at the doors around a poster of the main event, a trapeze artist called Jules Léotard. It didn't look promising, but Fin went up to the doorman and asked if he knew an actress by the name of Kaminski. 'No actresses here,' he said. 'We only got acrobats and dancers.' He suggested they try the Adelphi on the Strand. 'They got melodramas showing, and some right good murders, I'm told.'

They headed east, through a maze of narrow backstreets. Suddenly, Fin had the feeling someone was watching her and she glanced around. Across the street, lit up by a gas lamp, was a picture of a haughty-looking woman plastered on the outside of a boarded-up shop. She had one eyebrow raised and her piercing eyes had been cleverly painted so that they seemed to be following the passers-by. Fin got hold of Eryk's sleeve and dragged him across the road for a closer look.

The poster was half hidden under all the advertisements for soap and corsets and toothache powders, but Fin could read her name – 'THE BARONESS' – and she could see enough of her face to recognize the woman. 'It's her!' she said with certainty. 'It's Aunty Bashka.'

Eryk looked unconvinced. 'How are you sure of this?'

'I never forget a face,' Fin said, 'and she looks just the same as the girl in that picture we found in the attic.'

A scroll had been painted across the top of the poster, advertising the establishment where the woman was the star attraction. ' "Wilton's Music Hall",' she read. 'I know that place! It's down by the river.'

As she read on, Fin realized Aunty Bashka was not an actress, as Emily had said, but a medium.

'Listen to this,' she said, and she read aloud from the poster:

The Baroness is the unchallenged mistress of mesmerism. We can promise theatre-goers novel and breathtaking entertainment, along with stunning séances and ghostly encounters of every kind! Sixpence for the show, or two shillings with supper included.

She gave Eryk a nudge. 'Sounds brilliant, don't it?'

Eryk stared at the poster. 'Now I understand why Bashka is in disgrace.'

'Too right,' Fin said. 'You don't get many ladies from good families working in the music halls.'

Small was sitting in front of the picture of the Baroness wagging his tail, and Fin was encouraged to revise her earlier opinion of her aunt. After all, anyone that Lady Worth was ashamed of was bound to be worth knowing.

'We got more than enough money left for two tickets,' she said. 'I reckon things is looking up.'

18

Wilton's Music Hall was quite a distance away, in Shadwell, not far from Tobacco Dock, and by the time Fin and Eryk got there it was past seven o'clock.

Fin hid Small under her coat and went up to the ticket booth. 'Two for the Baroness,' she said.

The woman in the booth was counting the night's takings and didn't bother to look up. 'It's a full house tonight.'

'We're only small,' Fin said. 'You can squeeze us in.'

She glanced up and gave Fin and Eryk the once-over. 'It's not a children's show,' she told them. 'Anyway, it's nearly finished.'

Fin slammed a shilling on the counter. 'So? We're paying customers, ain't we?'

The ticket seller shrugged and took the money. 'Fair enough. You can stand in the gallery, at the back. And mind you go in quiet. We wouldn't want the spirits scared off,' she said with a smirk.

Fin and Eryk took their tickets, although when they got to the heavy velvet curtain that separated the auditorium from the lobby there was no one at the door to collect them and they went right in.

Fin had always wanted to see a show but had never had the money, and she looked eagerly around. The auditorium was dim, but as her eyes adjusted, the press of people, the polished wood and rich upholstery, the crystal chandeliers that hung from the ceilings all emerged from the gloom. She could feel the tense atmosphere of the place, which made her flush hot with excitement.

Despite what the ticket seller said about standing at the back, Fin grabbed hold of Eryk's sleeve and pushed through to the balcony at the edge of the gallery, where they had a good view of the stage. The only light in the auditorium came from there – a single candle burning on the table at which the Baroness sat, her head covered in a gauzy shroud. The place was packed, but no one spoke or coughed or fidgeted about. All was keen expectation, and the audience seemed to be leaning forward, hanging over the balcony, perched on the very edge of their seats.

Then the Baroness held up her hand. It was caught in the candlelight, which threw an enlarged six-fingered silhouette on to the back wall. The crowd *oohed* and *aahed* at the sight. Fin glanced at Eryk and he nodded – she had been right, there was no doubt the Baroness was a Kaminski.

Now the Baroness lowered her hand, moving it slowly in a circle over the candle's flame. 'Is there a spirit present?' She had an accent like Eryk's, which made Fin warm to her straight away.

As she spoke, the candle flame rose up and the table began to judder, to gasps from the audience. The Baroness stood and opened her arms. She tilted her face up and the shroud slid from her head to the floor. 'Come, good spirits of the dead,' she whispered. 'We are waiting for you!'

For a moment, nothing happened and all was silent. Then a faint sound began to emerge. It grew louder and louder, and Fin and Eryk screwed up their faces as it rose to an ear-splitting screech. In the gloom above the Baroness's head a violin appeared, its bow drawn across the strings by an unseen hand. A shudder travelled through the audience and the woman standing next to Fin let out a moan and buried her face in her companion's shoulder.

As if the sound caused her pain, the Baroness pressed her hands to her ears and began to writhe about, 'Please . . .' she cried, holding her hands out to the crowd, 'I need your help. These are not good spirits who have come here tonight! If you wish to live, join your hands and sing!'

In the pit, a lamp came on and an organ began to play 'Stand Up, Stand Up for Jesus'. The audience got to their feet and began to sing in uncertain, quavering voices. Fin knew it was all a trick, but she joined in the fun, singing at the top of her voice. Meanwhile, the spectral violin swooped about, now joined by a host of blasting trumpets and booming drums, creating a hideous cacophony of sound.

'Louder!' the Baroness demanded. 'Sing louder or we are lost!'

The audience redoubled their efforts, belting out the hymn in passionate voices. Above the Baroness's head a band of heavenly cherubs appeared in the darkness and set about the ghostly orchestra, smiting them with arrows from their bows. Fin cheered them on, but when she glanced at Eryk she was amused to find he had his eyes squeezed shut and was gripping the balustrade in terror.

The battle raged throughout the hymn, but during the last verse the cherubs got the upper hand. The spectators were encouraged and some even sank to their knees to give thanks. At last, the discordant sound of the ghostly orchestra faded, and as the final notes of the hymn rang out, the instruments and the cherubs disappeared.

The Baroness came to stand at the edge of the stage. 'We have defeated them together!' she cried. 'Have no fear, for good shall always conquer evil.' She gave a deep bow and as the velvet curtains on either side of the stage began to close, she vanished in a puff of smoke.

For a moment, the auditorium was plunged into darkness and there were a few panicky screams before the lights came up and the audience cheered and clapped.

Fin turned to Eryk. His eyes were open now, but his face was fixed in shock. 'Come on,' she said. 'Let's get backstage before the rush.'

Eryk nodded distractedly. 'Have never seen anything like this,' he murmured.

Fin smiled. 'Well worth a shilling. What did you think, Small?' But Small was curled up in Fin's coat, fast asleep.

While the rest of the audience were still applauding, they went downstairs. Here, the wealthy supper crowd were getting up from long tables that were still laden with the remains of their dinners. Fin and Eryk made their way to the exit beside the stage and slipped through. They squeezed past two boys who were lowering a cupid and the trumpets from the gallery with a winch. Eryk stopped to look, open-mouthed. 'So . . . it was not real . . .'

Fin laughed and rolled her eyes. 'It's only a show! You are funny, Eryk.'

Around the back, they found the Baroness's dressing room. A small crowd were gathered outside, held back by a burly doorman with impressive sideburns. They pushed their way through to the front and Fin waved at the doorman to catch his attention.

'What d'you want?' he said.

'To see the Baroness.'

'I bet you do!' He tucked his hands behind his back and rocked back and forth on his heels. 'You and half of London.'

'But she'll want to see me,' Fin said. 'I'm her niece.'

The man peered at her second-hand dress and cap and smirked. 'You got to be joking. The Baroness is a *lady.* She's hardly likely to have a ragamuffin like you for a relative. Now clear off, the pair of you.'

Fin really didn't like to use the name, but she had no choice. 'Tell her –' she squeezed her eyes shut to make saying it less awful – 'tell her that Magdalena Kaminski is here to see her.'

The man huffed in disbelief, but he knocked at the dressing-room door and, on receiving a reply, went in. A few seconds later the door flew open and the doorman was bundled out, closely followed by the Baroness herself.

She looked a state. Her hair was stuck to her head and covered in netting and half her face was still plastered in thick paint. Her gaze jumped from Eryk to Fin and back again. Even under all that stage make-up, Fin could see she'd gone pale.

She turned to the doorman. 'I think you'd better fetch me a brandy, Sam.'

Fin was surprised that the woman's voice didn't have a trace of the Polish accent she'd had onstage. 'And get rid of all these people,' she said, gesturing to the gathered crowd.

Now, her gaze settled on Small, curled up in Fin's coat, and her mouth fell open. 'Goodness me,' she said, 'is that Hercules?'

Fin was about to say her dog didn't answer to that name, when to Fin's surprise, Small woke up, yipped happily and leaped into the woman's arms. She let him lick her face and laughed when he sneezed. 'What is it?' she said. 'Don't you like the taste of stage paint? Luckily, I have a bit of leftover steak pie, which I'm absolutely certain will have a better flavour.'

She ushered them all into her dressing room and made them sit down on a pink velvet sofa while she put a slice of pie on a saucer and put it down on the floor for Small. Then she sat down at a dressing table strewn with sticks of make-up, garish pieces of paste jewellery and the wig she must have been wearing during the performance.

Up close, she had none of the aristocratic haughtiness she'd had in the publicity poster, or even on the stage.

'Are you really a baroness?' Fin asked.

Her aunt raised an eyebrow. 'My title is as genuine as my ability to speak with the dead,' she said. Then she turned to Eryk. 'And who are you, young man?'

Eryk got up, made a low bow and introduced himself as Bashka's cousin. 'And I like very much your show,' he added.

'Thank you, Eryk, I'm glad to hear it.' Now she looked at Fin and a frown appeared between her painted brows. 'It is wonderful to see you both here, but after all these years . . . I can hardly believe it. Are you really Magdalena?'

'Oh yes.' Fin laid her right hand in her lap, deliberately spreading out her six fingers for her aunt to see. 'But I only answer to Fin.'

'Fin?'

'Short for Fingers.'

'Yes, of course.' Aunty Bashka began to twist a delicate ring on her own sixth finger which, Fin saw, was engraved with the family crest. 'I only saw you once before,' she said. 'You were a baby then, but I remember you shared the family trait . . . and I remember your hair.' She looked pointedly at the cap Fin was wearing and Fin tugged it off, letting her long red hair fall down over her shoulders.

Her aunt blinked tears away. 'You really are her. You really are little Magdalena.' She stretched out her six-fingered hand and Fin did the same, linking her extra little finger with Bashka's.

'*Lojalność*,' they said together.

'How come you sound so different onstage?' Fin asked.

Aunty Bashka laughed. 'Oh that! I lost my Polish twang long ago, but I like to put it on for the show. For some reason, people believe that aristocrats with accents are more in touch with the spirit world.'

'You ain't ashamed of being Polish then?' Fin said.

Her aunt looked surprised by the question. 'Of course not, I was born there . . .' She raised an eyebrow and then a look of understanding spread across her face. 'Ah, I think you may have met my older sister, Lady Worth?'

Fin nodded.

Aunty Bashka smiled. 'Unlike her, I am proud to be called Kaminski and I love my homeland . . . but I am also rather fond of London. Come,' she said. 'I am sure you have much to tell me. Let's go back to my house and have some supper.'

There was always a hansom cab waiting to take the Baroness home after the show, driven by Charlie, an old friend. His horse, Maisie, was nothing like Dr Hunt's terrifying steed, and he let Eryk and Fin make a fuss of her, patting her neck and stroking her soft nose.

'You got a friend for life there,' Charlie said as Fin fed Maisie the carrot he'd given her.

The cab was really only meant for two, but the three of them managed to squeeze in. Fin had never been in a hansom cab (she didn't count the journey in Lady Worth's carriage, which was grander but far less enjoyable). 'This is brilliant,' she said, pressing her nose to the glass. 'We're going so fast it's like we're flying. Snot would love this. If only him and George could see me now!'

Charlie stopped at a fried fish shop on the way, and Eryk got out to collect their supper. When Bashka and Fin were alone, Fin told her aunt how she'd come to be a leecher, having been left on Ma Stump's doorstep.

'Wrapped in newspaper?' Aunty Bashka shook her head. 'I don't understand it. Why would Marta do such a thing?'

'Oh . . .' Fin's shoulders fell in disappointment. 'I was hoping you'd be able to tell me that.'

Bashka took Fin's hand. 'There must have been a good reason. She loved you, I am sure of that.' She bit her lip. 'What was it like, living with this . . . Ma Stump, was it?'

Fin could see that telling her aunt about the bad things would help no one. 'Well . . .' She shrugged. 'It were always lively.'

Eryk returned with their supper and they continued their journey, soon arriving at the small house that Bashka rented on one of the more respectable squares near the Regent's Park.

As they got out of the cab and went up the steps to the front door, Fin heard music coming from within.

'Come and meet Amelia Carmichael, my companion and spirit accomplice.' Bashka led them upstairs to a parlour where an elegant young woman was sitting at a piano. She played a final chord, then lifting her hands from the keys she turned towards them. 'Hello?' she said. 'Who's this?'

'This is Eryk,' Bashka said, 'a cousin from Poland. And this is my niece Fin, Marta's daughter.'

The woman's eyes widened and she and Bashka exchanged a glance. 'Oh! How unexpected!' She got up and shook Fin and Eryk's hands. 'I'm Amelia. Delighted to make your acquaintance.'

They all sat down in front of the fire to eat their supper. Small was already full of pie, but he somehow managed to snaffle down a little bit of everyone's fish before he curled up on Fin's lap and fell asleep. Amelia said she wasn't hungry, but she lounged on the arm of Bashka's chair and kept leaning over and pinching her food. She asked a lot of questions and soon discovered Eryk came from the Carpathian Mountains. 'How wonderful,' she said. 'I am a keen fell-walker, you know.'

Eryk perked up. 'I too. I wish to be mountain climber one day.' The pair of them spent the rest of the meal in a lively discussion that took in the grandeur of the Alps, Amelia's long-held desire to climb Mont Blanc, and the best clothing to wear at altitude.

'Now,' Bashka said when they'd finished eating. 'What I haven't yet discovered is how the two of you found me.'

Fin exchanged a rueful glance with Eryk. She was back on home turf, stuffed full and warm in the parlour of a woman who was the talk of the town, and, more importantly, a relative who was clearly pleased to have been found by the two of them. It made everything that had happened at Castle Kaminski feel very far away, like a bad dream.

Still, it was impossible to forget why they had come. Fin licked the last of the salt and grease off her fingers and recounted the whole story, from the time Lady Worth spotted her six-fingered hand in the Tripe and Eel, to her and Eryk's arrival at Wilton's Music Hall. Bashka glanced at Amelia at the mention of Dr Hunt and clutched a hand to her heart when Fin told her about meeting the Countess in Emily's room.

Fin peered at her anxiously. 'You do believe us, don't you?'

'Oh yes,' her aunt said. 'I met the Countess once myself.'

'When?' Eryk asked.

'It was back in the old country, when I was a bit younger than you. It was just as you describe. She made me tell her things and it felt as if she tore my heart to shreds and twisted what was left round her fingers.' She shivered. 'I will never be able to forget the stink of her. That's why we left our home in Poland. It was to escape from her.'

She got up and paced back and forth in front of the fire. 'So Marta was right.'

Fin looked up sharply. 'Right about what?'

'She was certain the Countess had followed us here, to England.' She glanced at Fin, whose heart was beating so hard she thought she might explode. 'I wonder if Marta discovered that Doctor Hunt was a familiar? Lady Worth was newly widowed and he was hanging around her even then.' She narrowed her eyes. 'I thought him no worse than any of the other entitled prigs my sister liked to surround herself with.' She shook her head. 'But to think what he did to poor Penelope . . .' She punched her fist into her open palm, a gesture Fin was sure Lady Worth would consider most unladylike, and which made her like Aunty Bashka even more. 'But I will not let the same thing happen to Emily, I promise you that.'

'You have plan?' Eryk asked.

Bashka stared off into the distance. 'Lady Worth and I are estranged and I left Castle Kaminski many years ago, determined never to return, but this news means I must go back.' She pressed her lips together. 'I will go tomorrow, first thing, and I'll make that stubborn sister of mine face the truth.'

Eryk looked unconvinced. 'I try already.' He gestured to Fin. 'We both try.'

Fin nodded in agreement. 'It won't be easy,' she said. 'That Doctor Hunt's got Lady Worth wrapped round his little finger.'

For a while they all stared glumly into the fire, until Amelia said moping never helped anything, and she started up a heated discussion with Eryk about crampons.

While they were talking, Bashka led Fin over to the other side of the room where a number of photographs, including several of Amelia in her walking outfits, were arranged in silver frames on a marble-topped sideboard. 'Look,' she said, picking up a picture. 'Here's one of me and Marta, before we came to England.'

It wasn't very clear, but Fin could see two young girls with their arms round each other's waist. The picture was tantalizing and the thought that her mother and Bashka had been close made her wish all the more that she could have known her. 'What was she like?'

Her aunt smiled, remembering her sister, as she told her about Marta's sweet tooth and her passion for poppy-seed cake, her love of horses and, of course, dogs. 'She kept several Jack Russells, but Hercules – I mean Small – was her favourite.' Aunty Bashka went on to describe the arguments Fin's mother used to have with Mrs Benton over hygiene and Small sleeping on the bed.

Fin laughed. 'She said the same to me!'

'Marta was loving and loyal,' her aunt continued more sadly. 'And she was determined and brave, like any true Kaminski.' She bowed her head. 'I miss her every day.'

'What do you think happened?' Fin asked. 'Lady Worth said she drowned, but she wouldn't tell me any more.'

'I cannot blame her for that.' She sighed and ran a hand over her hair. 'It is not a pretty story. She was found at low tide by mudlarks on the banks of the Thames near Deptford. I will never forget that day. It was pouring with rain and they had laid her out on the wharf. I couldn't believe she'd gone. She looked so perfect. There wasn't a mark on her.'

'Then how did she get there?'

Bashka shook her head. 'I've asked myself the same question many times.' She glanced at Fin. 'At the inquest, the coroner said . . .' She clenched her fists, the knuckles whitening. 'Well . . . he suggested suicide, citing her grief over your poor father's death as the reason she took her own life. But I have never believed that. She loved you and had everything to live for. I have always suspected the Countess was involved, but I don't know how.'

Fin felt sure her aunt was right. Anger twisted up inside her and tightened like a knot.

Just then, the clock on the mantelpiece chimed the hour. 'Look at the time,' Bashka said. 'Amelia, it's nine o'clock – we must get ready, my client will soon be arriving.'

'What sort of client?' Eryk asked.

Amelia smiled as she headed for the door. 'The sort who wishes to speak with the dead.'

'You mean a séance?' Fin perked up. 'Can we come?'

Her aunt nodded. 'I don't see why not.'

'Will it be like music hall,' Eryk asked, 'with violins and trumpets?'

Bashka raised an eyebrow. 'Not as much drama as that, but I can promise you all manner of eerie sounds and visions – provided by Amelia, of course. But first, I must get ready.' She went out and came back a moment later wearing a sparkling tiara. 'The clients love a bit of glamour,' she said, eyeing herself in the mirror. 'How do I look?' She winked at Fin. 'Aristocratic enough?'

'Is it real?' Fin asked.

Bashka laughed. 'I wouldn't be doing this hocus-pocus if I could afford diamonds.'

Fin gazed at her aunt. She thought about the fried-fish supper, how they'd eaten it with their fingers, straight out of the newspaper. She couldn't imagine Bashka minding one way or the other about the polite way to eat soup and how Fin should hold her knife and fork. 'You're nothing like Lady Worth, are you?' she said.

The smile melted off Bashka's face. 'My older sister and I have never really got on. Your mother was in the middle, the glue that held the three of us together. Once she was gone, everything fell to pieces.'

'Come along,' Bashka said. 'We mustn't keep our guests waiting.'

She led them downstairs to a room that had evidently been set aside for ghostly encounters, and decorated to match. Heavy velvet hangings fell in swathes from the ceiling, giving the room the feel of a luxurious and rather glamorous tent. The drama was heightened by a single candelabra, which deepened the shadows lurking beyond its faltering circle of light. Set in the middle of all the drapery was a small round table covered in a cloth, with a huge ornate mirror tilted above it, so that the table and everything on top was reflected in the glass.

As they went in, Amelia was seating the clients: a middle-aged woman whose dress and bonnet were heaving with frills and bows, and her daughter, whose clothing was so simple it seemed to have been purposely chosen to contrast with her mother's.

'Good evening, Mrs Grey.' Bashka was in character as the Baroness again and spoke with the same accent she'd used onstage at the music hall. 'May I introduce my niece and my young cousin? They will be assisting me this evening.'

'What?' Mrs Grey held a jewelled lorgnette to her face and peered through the lenses at Fin and Eryk. 'But they're children!'

'Children are often the most sensitive,' the Baroness said, seating herself at the table and motioning for Fin and Eryk to do the same. 'Do you not see their auras?'

Mrs Grey screwed her eyes up behind her glasses. 'Oh . . . ah, yes . . . most colourful.'

The Baroness bowed her head in acknowledgement. 'I knew you would. I've often said you have the gift yourself.'

'Well, I can't see anything,' the daughter said, looking from Eryk to Fin. 'They look like normal children to me.'

'Oh, do be quiet, Felicity.' Mrs Grey turned to the Baroness. 'Unfortunately, she takes after her father – he had all the spiritual sensitivity of a coal scuttle.'

The Baroness smothered a smile and changed the subject. 'May I offer some fortifying refreshments before we begin?' She called Amelia forward to serve the two ladies. Although the brew was poured from a teapot into china cups and saucers, Fin noticed that it smelled just like gin and lemon.

'So, how shall we proceed this evening, ladies?' the Baroness asked.

Mrs Grey pressed a ring-laden hand to her throat. 'I should like to hear from my darling Sebastian as to his comforts. Is he warm enough? Is he having nourishing meals? Is he taking regular exercise?'

Fin was wondering what kind of a person Sebastian had been, when the Baroness asked Mrs Grey if she had brought any personal effects and she handed over a dog collar.

The Baroness took it and stood up. 'Shall we begin?' She signalled to Amelia, who cleared the cups from the table. When Amelia had left the room, the Baroness blew all the candles out but one.

Straight away, the atmosphere seemed to shift, and although Fin knew it was only a pantomime, she couldn't help a shudder running through her body.

The Baroness removed the tablecloth. Underneath, the edge of the wooden top was inlaid with the letters of the alphabet. She put an empty wine glass upside down in the middle. 'You should not try to move the glass,' she said, 'but neither should you prevent its movement. The spirits will cause the glass to move, and in this way your dearly departed will communicate with us directly.'

'Let's hope Sebastian is a good speller,' Felicity said under her breath.

The Baroness ignored the interruption and placed her sixth finger on the bowl of the glass. 'I and my niece and cousin shall use our spirit fingers; you ladies may use any finger you choose.'

When everyone had placed a finger on the glass, the Baroness tilted her head back. 'Sebastian, are you there?' she whispered.

For a moment, nothing happened. The only sounds were the breathing of the participants and, drifting in from outside, the faint cries of night hawkers selling their wares on the streets. The knocking started up so suddenly that Mrs Grey let out a cry and even Felicity jumped. It seemed to be coming from underneath the table.

'Sebastian,' the Baroness intoned, 'are you with us?'

She was answered by the barking of a dog, or, as Fin suspected, Amelia pretending to be a dog from a hiding place behind the velvet hangings. The table quivered and the glass began to move, travelling round the edge of the table until it had completed a full circle. Then it sped up, swooping from one side to the other, from letter to letter:

Happy Chasing Rabbits

Fin glanced at Mrs Grey and her daughter to see how they were taking this development; Felicity looked bored, but her mother was entranced.

'Oh, my dear, dear Sebastian! It is such a relief to know you're happy and well.'

This was answered by a series of yaps, and Mrs Grey gasped.

'I felt his little paw, just then, upon my shoulder. I would know his touch anywhere. Ask him, Baroness, is he getting enough to eat?'

The glass whizzed about the table again:

Steak and Gravy Every Day

'That was always his favourite,' Mrs Grey whispered.

There were further messages from beyond, concerning sausages, walkies and squirrels, until finally Sebastian said it was time for his nap. There was a snuffling sound, a few more yips, and then Amelia came in with a fresh pot of 'tea' and the séance was over.

'*Now* do you believe me?' Mrs Grey asked Felicity. 'Only my own dear Sebastian could have given those answers.'

'Indeed,' Felicity replied. 'There can't be another dog in London who eats sausages and chases squirrels.'

When the two ladies had finished their drinks and Amelia had shown them out, Fin said, 'That was even better than your show, Aunty. You got that Mrs Grey eating out your hand.'

Bashka mock-curtsied. 'Why, thank you.'

'How did you manage the paw on the shoulder?' Fin asked.

Her aunt pursed her lips. 'I really shouldn't give away my stage secrets, but Amelia is a genius with a bit of fur and a stick.'

Eryk nodded thoughtfully. 'You have that lady in frills convinced, but her daughter not so much.'

Bashka tapped the envelope Mrs Grey had left on the table. 'It's not the daughter who's paying.'

Suddenly, a breath of freezing air came into the room, making everyone shudder. Bashka drew her shawl closer round her shoulders. 'Amelia must have left the front door open –' but before she could finish speaking, the candle flames shivered.

Fin glanced at her aunt, expecting her to wink at this new trick, but Bashka's face was a picture of astonishment as, one by one, the candles were snuffed out by invisible fingers and the room was plunged into darkness.

'I am not finding this so funny, Cousin,' Eryk said.

'I assure you, it's not me!' came Bashka's quavering reply. 'Amelia!' she called out. 'Bring a lamp at once!'

A dim glow appeared in the room, but it was not Amelia, or a lamp. There was a new presence here – Fin could feel it. It emanated from the mirror that hung over the table, tilted above them. The room was now in darkness, yet in the mirror's reflection Fin could clearly see the table at which they sat. She could see her own terrified face, as well as Eryk's and Bashka's, reflected in the glass. And next to Fin, where Felicity had been, another shimmering face appeared.

Fin watched, too frightened to move, as the reflection of a shining six-fingered hand reached out of the darkness and took hold of Fin's, linking their extra little fingers together. She would have leaped up from the table, but now the only part of Fin that was able to move was the hand that was gripped by the apparition. Against her will, it was forced on to the table and pressed against the bowl of the wine glass. Eryk and Bashka must have been paralysed with fear too, for the only thing that moved in the dark, silent room was the glass. It slid across the tabletop from letter to letter, spelling out its ghostly message in the mirror:

DO NOT DENY WHO YOU ARE
YOU ARE MAGDALENA KAMINSKI
THE GIRL WITH HER HEAD ON FIRE
YOU MUST FIND THE LAIR
OF THE STRZYGA
YOU MUST DESTROY HER

Fin gazed up at the shining reflected face. 'Who are you?' she said.

At once, the glass began to slide round the edge of the table again.

MY NAME IS NATASHA
SEEK ME IN THE MIRROR
FIND ME IN THE BOOK

21

The apparition faded. The wine glass came to a halt and Fin's hand was released.

'Who was that?' Fin said, turning to Eryk. 'Who is Natasha?'

Eryk glanced at Bashka, whose face was frozen in shock. 'Every Kaminski know of her,' he said to Fin. 'She was Countess's daughter, and first victim.'

'The Countess stole her memories?'

Eryk nodded. 'Countess murder her, use her life to become *strzyga*.'

Just then Amelia came in with a lamp, whistling cheerfully. 'What's this, all sitting in the dark?' She glanced from one face to another. 'You lot look like you've seen a ghost.'

'I don't suppose there's any of that tea left?' Bashka said in a wobbly voice.

Amelia poured out what was left and Bashka swigged it down in one, before explaining to Amelia what had happened. 'I suppose I shouldn't be surprised,' she said. 'If there's *strzyga*, why wouldn't there be ghosts?'

Eryk nudged Fin with his elbow. 'See? Is what I say.'

Fin rubbed her six-fingered hand. It was still numb and cold as a block of ice. 'The girl with her head on fire,' she said, 'that's what Eryk says . . . and it's what *she* called me too.'

'Who?' her aunt asked.

'The Countess, in Emily's bedroom, soon as she set eyes on me.'

Bashka exchanged a worried glance with Eryk. 'Oh no . . .'

'What d'you mean?' Fin said. Eryk had told her about the legend of the girl with her head on fire, but in all the excitement she hadn't given it another thought. 'It ain't that bad, is it?'

Eryk and her aunt exchanged another glance.

Fin tutted. 'And you can stop doing that an' all. Just tell me.'

'Of course you're right,' Aunty Bashka said. 'There is an old story in the *History of the Kaminskis*, about a girl with red hair. The story says that she is the one who will destroy the Countess or –'

She stopped abruptly and a jolt of dread ran down Fin's spine.

'Or what?' She looked from Eryk to her aunt, who both avoided her eye and stared down at the table. 'Or be destroyed, is that it?' Fin narrowed her eyes at Eryk. 'Why didn't you tell me that bit before?'

Eryk looked guilty. 'It was night and we are scared already. I do not want to make worse.'

'Come on now,' Amelia said. 'You're safe with us. And anyway, no one knows you're here.'

'They will soon,' Fin said. 'As soon as Aunty Bashka shows herself at Castle Kaminski tomorrow to talk to Lady Worth, she and everyone else'll know it was us what put her up to it. They'll know we're here in her house.'

Bashka bit her lip. 'I'm afraid so, but remember: a *strzyga* may not enter without being invited in.'

Fin was glad to hear it, but she knew that the Countess had her familiars and Fin had a feeling the same rule would not apply to them. She didn't feel very safe any more. 'So what happened to Natasha?' she asked.

Her aunt sighed. 'As Eryk said, she was the Countess's first victim. Her story is in the book.'

Fin remembered the message Natasha had spelled out: *Find me in the book.* She was beginning to see why Eryk thought the *History of the Kaminskis* was so important. 'Have you got it – the book, I mean?'

Aunty Bashka nodded. 'And you shall see it, but not tonight. It's nearly midnight. We must make the house safe and there is much to do.'

Bashka made up beds for Fin, Eryk and Small on the sofas in the drawing room, while Amelia brought them cups of hot sugared milk, which she said was an excellent cure for shock. Once Fin and Eryk were settled, Bashka and Amelia went around the house, checking all the doors and windows were locked and stuffing any cracks with newspaper. Fin listened to their soft comforting voices, until at last they finished their task and went to bed themselves.

Fin lay in the darkness with Small curled up in her arms. *The girl with her head on fire* . . . She squeezed her eyes shut. How was she supposed to know what to do? She didn't want to be the one who had to save everyone or, worse, be destroyed herself while trying. Why couldn't it be someone else's destiny?

'You still awake?' she whispered to Eryk.

'Yes.'

'Are you . . . afraid?'

'Of course. You?'

'Yes, very . . . You know, I just don't think I'm up to it.'

'Why?'

Fin sighed. 'It ought to be someone cleverer than me.'

Eryk huffed. 'You are clever enough.'

Fin knew Eryk was right – it wasn't any lack of cleverness she was really worried about, it was something much more shameful. 'Braver than me then,' she said at last. 'See, I were always brought up to run at the first sign of trouble.'

Eryk sat up. 'Not true. You face the doctor on the marshes and you put yourself in danger for Emily.'

Fin remembered cowering under Emily's bed, trying to stop her ears and pretend none of it was happening. 'I nearly didn't though,' she admitted.

'Who cares about *nearly*?' Eryk said. 'Is what you actually do that counts.'

When Fin replied, her voice was small. 'I'm 'fraid I'm more like Ma Stump than a Kaminski. I were raised on her upside-down ideas of right and wrong. I'm 'fraid I'll let everyone down.'

'No, I trust you,' Eryk said. 'And you are not alone. Bashka and Amelia will help. I will help.'

Fin wanted to believe him, but it was all so differcnt from what she'd grown up to expect. At Ma's, a person survived by earning money, or at least by making themselves useful. Her only true friends, the only ones who'd looked out for her, had been Snot and Small.

'But why would you do that?' she asked him. 'Why would you put yourself in danger for me?'

'Because it is right thing to do,' he said indignantly. 'Same reason you do for Emily. You are cousin and member of Kaminski family.'

Fin couldn't help smiling. She'd only known Eryk for a few days, but already she thought this was typical. He was so . . . she searched for the right word, but could only come up with the Kaminski motto: *loyal.*

'My mother taught me this,' Eryk continued. 'We are all suffering same curse, same fear. You are the one who will free us from this, and I will do anything to help you, because we are family.'

Fin was glad it was dark; it meant Eryk couldn't see the tears that rolled down her cheeks and soaked into Small's soft ears. *Family.* She turned the word over in her head. It was all she had ever wanted, to be part of something, to be cared for, to have a family who loved her. She'd wanted to find her mother, but, instead, Emily and Eryk and her aunt Bashka and Amelia had appeared – a girl with no memory, a cousin from Poland, a fake spirit medium and her piano-playing accomplice! They weren't the kind of family she had originally hoped for or could have even imagined.

She'd also discovered another aunt, Lady Worth, who had been ashamed of her and had made no secret of it. At Castle Kaminski, Fin had been expected to change, to learn to be a lady. Here at Aunty Bashka's, it was different. Despite the way she had been dragged up by Ma, Bashka had been overjoyed to find out Fin was her long-lost niece.

Fin thought about the wonderful evening they had all spent together, eating greasy fried fish out of newspaper in front of the fire. No one had seemed to care how she ate or how she spoke. Fin dried her tears. Maybe, just maybe, she'd found people, a family, who wouldn't want to change her, who would care about her enough to accept her just as she was.

But now she knew without a doubt that being part of this family came at a price. She could no longer deny the truth: she was the girl with her head on fire. Eryk and Aunty Bashka had said it, the Countess and now Natasha had said the same. It was her duty, as a Kaminski, to do everything she could to find the Countess's lair and destroy her.

Her mind circled back to her new family, the people who, although she'd only just met them, she was certain she could learn to love. But even these warm and wonderful thoughts could not lift the pall of dread that lay heavy on her heart.

The next morning, after a breakfast of hot buttered muffins, Aunty Bashka took Fin up to the drawing room.

'A carriage is coming to take me to Castle Kaminski,' she said. 'It'll be here any minute, but first, as I promised, I will show you the book.'

She unlocked a drawer in the sideboard, took out an old leather-bound tome and handed it to Fin. 'This is it, *History of the Kaminskis*. It's written in Polish, but Eryk will read it to you.'

Fin opened the book and the ancient smell of dust escaped from the pages. Fin flicked through. 'I never heard of a family having their own history book,' she said.

'The Kaminskis have always written everything down. We have to – we are a family who cannot trust our memory, and bad things happen if we allow ourselves to forget.'

Fin glanced up at her. 'You mean Lady Worth, don't you?'

Aunty Bashka sighed. 'I only hope I can convince her about Doctor Hunt and the Countess. Emily's life depends on it.'

She led Fin over to the sofa and they sat down together. 'I'm sorry I have to go. I should like nothing better than to sit here with you and Eryk and explore our history together.' She smiled, and Fin noticed the fine lines round her eyes, the deep shadows that could not be hidden with face powder.

'You look ever so tired,' Fin said. 'Bet you didn't get much sleep last night.'

'Did anyone?' Bashka laughed, but then immediately turned serious. 'I was thinking about Marta. What you said yesterday in the cab – how she'd left you on that doorstep, wrapped in nothing but newspaper . . .' She shook her head. 'I couldn't understand it, but after what happened last night, I think perhaps I do.'

'It's about me being that girl, the one with her head on fire, isn't it?'

Her aunt nodded. 'We all knew the story, of course, but the legend is hundreds of years old and I suppose no one put two and two together. Except Marta. She must have realized, and was trying to hide you from the Countess.' She took Fin's hands and looked into her eyes. 'I know my sister. She would never willingly have left you and it's the only thing that makes sense. She left you in a place no one would ever think to look. It explains the newspaper too – if you'd been wearing fine clothes, people would've seen you were no ordinary foundling.'

'Surely she would've told *someone*,' Fin said.

'But who? If she had told anyone, the Countess would have hunted them down and taken their memory of where you were. It must have been a terrible choice, but it was the only way to keep you safe.'

Fin thought for a moment. 'It still don't explain how she ended up in the Thames, though, do it?'

The room suddenly felt cold and Aunty Bashka shivered. She took a log from the basket and threw it into the grate. Neither of them spoke and the only sound was the roar of the flames as the fire took hold.

'Where is she now?' Fin asked. 'Where did you bury her?'

'The family mausoleum in Highgate Cemetery.' Seeing the sadness in Fin's face, her aunt took her hand.

'As soon as I return, we will go there together and pay our respects.'

From downstairs they heard the sound of the door knocker and Eryk shouted up the stairs.

'That's my carriage.' Aunty Bashka hugged and kissed her. 'I can't tell you how happy I am that you and Eryk and Small are here, Fin. Now listen. I'll be as quick as I can, but I'm bound to be gone for a few days. Amelia will look after you. Don't go out, and keep the windows shut at night.'

When Bashka had gone, Fin opened the book again. As her aunt had said, it was handwritten in Polish, but the words were interweaved with illuminated images that Fin had no difficulty understanding. In the flyleaf was a picture of a girl whose long red hair was like a fire. The flames spread out around her, curling over the text, while above her a bright full moon rose in the night sky. On the opposite page stood a woman in a black dress with dark hair and burning eyes.

Fin flicked ahead. The Countess appeared on almost every page, surrounded by people Fin thought must be her Kaminski ancestors. It looked as if they had tried everything to defeat her. Some were shown gathering roots and herbs and brewing potions, while others had searched for the answer in books and scrolls; yet others had tried fighting her with swords. In despair, they turned their eyes up to heaven, their palms clasped together in prayer.

Nothing had worked. At the end of every chapter, there was the Countess, winding the golden threads of the Kaminski children's memories round and round her six-fingered hand. She was unstoppable. Maybe, Fin thought, this explained Lady Worth's attitude. After all, Fin knew herself how much easier it was to deny the truth than face up to failure.

When Eryk came into the drawing room, Fin flicked back through the pages to the illumination of the girl with her head on fire and pointed to the Polish text. 'What does this mean?' she asked.

Eryk took the book from her. 'It say, "Girl with head on fire must burn heart of *strzyga*. It is the only way."'

'Her heart? But how?'

Eryk shrugged. 'You must trust. When time come, you will know.'

Fin sighed. 'I don't see how we're going to manage it. Your family have been trying to defeat the Countess for years.'

He frowned at her. '*Our* family,' he corrected. 'Yes, will not be easy . . . but does not mean is not possible.' He weighed the book in his hand. 'Let us read of Natasha, Countess's daughter.'

Natasha's story was the first in the book. She told of her mother's beauty and her vanity, her terror of ageing, her obsession with discovering the secret of eternal youth. The Countess filled her court with alchemists and magicians and soothsayers who tempted her with prophecies of what she could be. As her mania took her deeper and deeper into dark magic, she learned to use her daughter's memories to make herself young again. But it was never enough, and she soon realized that she needed to take Natasha's whole mind and, with it, her life itself.

At first, the Countess could not bring herself to commit such a heinous act, to murder her own child. But each time she stole another piece of her daughter's mind, it became a little easier.

'Who wrote this?' Fin asked.

'Legend say it was her nurse. She try to help Natasha while she was alive, and she wrote her story when she die.'

Eryk continued reading. According to the book, the Countess had one weakness. ' "There is one memory the Countess can never do away with," ' Eryk translated. ' "It is the memory of a mother who sacrificed her child for vanity, for herself. She bears shame and suffers for what she has done to her own daughter." '

As Eryk read to Fin, there came a knock at the front door. Amelia called out from downstairs that she would answer it. A few minutes later, she came rushing into the drawing room, breathless.

'What's the matter?' Fin said.

'I have just had this telegraphic message from my father,' Amelia said, waving the paper she was holding. 'My little brother Edward – he's fallen ill. I must go to them immediately, only . . .' she looked from Fin to Eryk.

'Do not be worrying about us,' Eryk said.

'I would take you with me,' Amelia replied, 'but they suspect typhoid fever and I can't put you two in danger.'

The thought of Amelia leaving them alone in the house made Fin's stomach clench with fear, but she covered it with a smile and nodded in agreement. 'We can look after ourselves,' she said as confidently as she could.

Amelia clasped her hands together. 'But I promised Bashka I wouldn't let you out of my sight.'

'Sounds like Edward and your dad need you,' Fin said. 'You've got to go.'

'Yes,' Amelia said. 'Of course . . . you're right. I'll go and pack.'

Before Amelia left, she made Fin and Eryk promise not to leave the house or answer the door. 'I'll send word to the Baroness, tell her to hurry back as soon as possible.' She pressed a scrap of paper into Fin's hand. 'My family's address in Surrey is there, if you need it. Now, is there anything I can do before I go?'

'You can stop worrying,' Fin said, leading her to the door. 'We'll be all right.'

They watched her climb up into the cab, her face a picture of anxiety as it pulled away.

When she'd gone, Fin and Eryk rushed back up to the drawing room and continued reading Natasha's story. She was finally murdered at the age of eleven, the time when, as the Countess discovered, a child's memories were at their most potent. The last thing Natasha's nurse wrote was the prophecy about the girl with her head on fire. Eryk translated as he read, and although the story was complicated, the message was clear. The memories of the girl with her head on fire would prove to be the most potent of all. They were so strong, they might help Fin defeat the Countess. But if she should fail, and the Countess was allowed to take her memories, the *strzyga* would gain the endless youth she craved and would no longer have to feed only on the children of her own descendants.

Fin turned to Eryk. 'You mean, she'll start feeding off *everyone*'s children, not just the Kaminskis?'

Eryk nodded. 'But listen – there is worse:

' "Those the Countess destroys shall find no rest. Not even in death. Girl with her head on fire must break the curse. For until she is defeated, Countess will continue to steal our memories, our lives, our very selves. We will be as nothing, for who are we if we cannot remember who we are?" '

Eryk put the book aside, and for a moment they sat with Natasha's question in silence.

'Is that why Natasha's a ghost?' Fin said. 'Cos she can't find no rest?'

Eryk nodded. 'Is not only our lives Countess takes. Is who we are. Our souls.'

Fin went over to the window and looked out. She could see a flower seller on the corner with a basket of red roses, calling to the passers-by and holding out her flowers to them. She wondered how people could be going about their lives as usual, when her own life had been rattled about and turned upside down.

She turned back to Eryk. 'So you're saying we've got to risk our lives – and not even just our lives, mind, but our bloomin' *eternal souls* – on the off-chance that we *might* be able to defeat a demon? A demon who has winged familiars pouring out her mouth, can paralyse a person, and turn herself to mist whenever she likes?'

Eryk frowned. 'You make it sound bad, but Countess is not indestructible, and prophecy say your memory will help.'

What he said was true. Fin had always known her memory was special and not like other people's. According to the book, she had the chance to defeat the demon who had blighted the Kaminskis for hundreds of years, but Fin was also the Countess's prime target, the means by which she hoped to gain eternal life. It all seemed impossible.

'But we don't know how to defeat her,' Fin said. 'We don't even know how to find her lair.'

Eryk shrugged. 'You are girl with head on fire. Answer will come.'

Fin picked at her fingernails. The idea of facing the Countess was terrifying, but what really frightened her was herself. Being brave and standing up for each other was something Eryk and the other Kaminskis had been taught from birth – they even had a special handshake to show the importance of loyalty. But Fin's upbringing had included none of that. Instead, she had been taught to look out only for herself. What if Ma Stump had ruined her with her upside-down version of right and wrong? What if she wasn't the right person for the job and ended up letting everyone down?

There was only one consolation in the whole terrible mess. At least now she knew why her mother had left her on Ma's doorstep. It was as Aunty Bashka guessed: her mother must have realized that Fin was the girl with her head on fire and so she had hidden her from the Countess – not because she didn't want her, but because she was trying to keep her safe from harm.

As she often did when she needed comfort, Fin returned to her most precious memory, the one that made her feel safe. She let her mind go back to the tenement leaning over the river. She could smell the stink of whale oil, and see the rickety steps that led up to Ma's attic as clear as if she were standing there. But the feeling of warmth and safety eluded her this time and the sense that she had once been loved refused to come.

She squeezed her eyes shut and tried again, but, with a rush of horror, she realized she could no longer remember her mother's face! And then Fin understood what story she must have told the Countess that night in Emily's bedroom; now she knew exactly which memory had been contained in the golden thread the *strzyga* wound round and round her fingers.

'I can't see her no more!' she opened her eyes and looked to Eryk. 'She's taken it! The Countess has stolen my mother from me!'

A searing wave of anger swept from her toes to the tip of her sixth finger and carried her fear away. Why did the Countess have to take *that* memory? Why not the one where Ma Stump had tried to sell her to Mr Canary? Why not the ones where Ma or George had teased her to the point of tears? Why not any one of the miserable times when she'd been hungry and cold? But no. The Countess had stolen away the memory that was most precious to her, the feeling that she had once been loved and the beautiful shining image of her mother's face.

23

'I'm goin' out,' Fin said as she ran down the stairs to the kitchen.

Small and Eryk followed close behind. 'Where?' Eryk called after her.

Fin took her cap off the peg and stuffed it on her head. 'Highgate Cemetery.'

'But we promise Amelia we stay here,' her cousin reminded her.

Fin pulled her coat on. 'I can't just sit here, Eryk. Don't you understand? The Countess has taken my mother away from me and I got to get her back.'

'How?'

'I don't know. But I feel like I've lost her, and I've got to find her again.'

'I understand.' Eryk took his coat off the peg and pulled it on. 'I come with you.'

Fin was about to say that he didn't understand, that no one could. But she remembered that Eryk's own parents had been dead for less than a year, and she realized that if anyone knew something about how she was feeling, it was him.

In case anyone was watching the house, the three of them went out through the back door and climbed over the garden wall. They made their way to the main road that went north to Highgate. Fin immediately felt better. She wasn't the sort of person who could sit about thinking. Visiting her mother's grave might be no help at all, but she needed to do something to try and get her mother back. She couldn't explain it, but she knew she needed to be close to her.

After a long uphill climb, they reached a gatehouse like a pair of medieval chapels with an archway through the middle.

'Is like something from history book,' Eryk said.

They went through the archway, which led them into the western half of the cemetery, and followed the paths that wound between the graves. Some were marked by plain stones or crosses made of granite and marble, while others were guarded by angels or topped with statues of dogs, lions and horses. There were many tombs and mausoleums that were truly grand, and when they reached Egyptian Avenue, they passed between a pair of towering stone obelisks and followed a path bordered by tombs with stone pillars at their doors that would have graced any manor house. It was a sunny day and the cemetery had something of the atmosphere of a pleasure park rather than a graveyard. There were a lot of people wandering about, clutching bouquets of flowers and visiting graves, but many did not wear black and seemed to have come there with the sole purpose of taking a pleasant afternoon stroll or to admire the fine views over the city.

Eryk was bemused by all this. 'Do English people worship death?' he asked.

'Only if they've got the money,' Fin said. She had seen many a pauper's grave in Hackney, where the bodies were thrown in together and there was nothing at all to mark who lay there.

The Kaminski mausoleum, when they eventually reached it, was no less lavish than the others in the cemetery. It was the size of a house, hexagonal and topped by a dome with stained glass windows depicting the family crest in each of the six sides. The whole structure was surrounded by gardens enclosed by a high wall. The entrance, an archway guarded by two stone angels, was sealed with a pair of wrought-iron gates. Fin pushed against them, but they were locked.

'Come on,' she said. 'Let's find a place to climb over.'

They all went round the side of the mausoleum, where they could not be seen from the path. There were handholds and footholds here and there, and Fin and Eryk were able to scramble up on to the top of the wall. Small could easily have squeezed through the bars of the gate to join them, but despite Fin calling him, he hung back and would not be persuaded.

Fin and Eryk climbed down into the garden of the mausoleum, or what must once have been a garden. Flower beds were marked out and rose bushes had been planted on either side of the path, but their stems were blighted and bare and nothing grew in the bare earth. There was no birdsong and the high walls cut the garden off from the outside, shading it from the sunlight. It was as if the place had been entirely given over to death and decay.

Fin and Eryk climbed the steps to a porch, passing between carved stone columns. Above the doorway was a marble scroll, engraved with the family name: KAMINSKI.

Fin stepped into a small hallway and Eryk followed. Ahead of them was another doorway that led to the heart of the tomb, a large chamber with a marble coffin standing on a plinth in the middle. High above their heads was a domed ceiling with six stone angels looking down. Dusty cobwebs hung from their wings, spanning the void between them.

Eryk examined the plaque attached to the marble coffin. 'Dorothea Kaminski,' he read, and he turned to Fin. 'She is your grandmother, my great-aunt.'

There were twelve doorways off the central chamber, six on either side, each leading to an individual tomb. Most were empty, but two had coffins inside. One belonged to Penelope Worth, the other to Marta Kaminski.

Eryk bowed his head when he saw the name. 'I go outside and wait for you there,' he said quietly.

When he'd gone, Fin walked around the tomb. The stonework of the coffin was already showing its age and a large crack ran across the lid. She read the inscription, which said Marta was a 'BELOVED SISTER AND MOTHER'. In an alcove behind the coffin stood a statue of a woman with a child in her arms. *That baby must be me!* Fin thought. She supposed it was because everyone had thought she too had drowned, that the two of them were in heaven together.

She squeezed her eyes shut and tried, once again, to retrieve her beloved memory, hoping the nearness to her mother might reawaken it. But it was useless. It had gone.

She closed her hands into fists as Natasha's words came back to her.

We will be nothing, for who are we if we cannot remember who we are?

Now she recognized the truth of those words. If Fin lost her memories, she would not be herself any more. Already she felt as if her heart had been picked over and torn apart, and for the first time she really understood the horror of what the Countess had taken from her.

One way or another, she must find the Countess's lair. She couldn't let this demon destroy the lives of all the Kaminskis and – if Fin did not stop her – the lives of many other children too.

She laid her six-fingered hand on the coffin's stone lid. 'It's me,' she said. 'Your daughter, Fin.' She glanced up at the statue, who looked back at her impassively. 'I expect you know me as Magdalena, and I know now that's who I really am. Only, that's a very long name for someone like me, and I haven't got used to it yet.'

It felt awkward talking to someone she didn't know, who was also dead and not likely to be listening. But Fin had things that needed to be said and so she cleared her throat.

'I used to be angry with you, for leaving me, for not coming back. But I want you to know I ain't angry with you any more, cos now I know you was trying to keep me safe.'

Fin knelt down in front of the statue of the mother and child. 'You done your best for me,' she said. 'And I'll do my best for you. I promise.'

Fin found Eryk and Small waiting on a bench outside the walls of the mausoleum. As soon as she appeared, Small rushed forward and jumped up, delighted to see her.

'You are all right?' Eryk asked.

'Yeah,' Fin said, leaning down to stroke Small. 'I'm glad I visited.' Being there had made Fin realize the weight she carried, not just for the Kaminskis, but for any child who might become a victim of the Countess.

As they wandered back to the gatehouse, Fin's mind turned to the child who, at that moment, was most in danger. 'I wonder if Aunty Bashka has made it to the castle yet . . . I hope Lady Worth listens this time, and gets rid of that horrible doctor, for Emily's sake.'

'I hope too. But is not all Lady Worth's fault.'

'Ain't it?'

'I do not think she is bad person. She is tricked by doctor. Familiars are good at hiding who they really are.'

'There must be some way of telling, though, don't you think?'

'Not by looks. The only thing they cannot hide is obsession for human blood.'

Fin nodded in agreement. 'Yeah, like the way the doctor insists on bleeding Emily every day and buying human-caught leeches what are full of blood . . .' A thought suddenly jumped into Fin's mind – she remembered the time she'd sold the very same human-caught leeches in the Tripe and Eel. 'Hang on a minute!' She grabbed Eryk's shoulder and pulled him round to face her. 'I know someone else who's obsessed by human blood.'

'Who?'

'Mr Canary. No wonder he was so keen to buy me off Ma!' She narrowed her eyes, remembering the way he'd sniffed at the tin of leeches like a bunch of flowers. 'I knew there was something wrong with him. You didn't like him either, did you, Small?'

Small gave a growl and two sharp barks in response.

'*And* he was the one what was buying human-caught leeches for Doctor Hunt, so they knows each other. Lady Worth weren't the only one what looked shocked about me having six fingers. You should've seen his face! I reckon he *knew* . . . he knew the Countess was looking for someone like me.'

'Where is this . . . Mr Canary?'

''Ere in London. He has an apothecary's shop in Holloway.' She nodded in satisfaction. 'Listen – do familiars visit their mistress?'

'Certainly.' Eryk raised an eyebrow. 'You think this can be way of finding Countess's lair?'

Fin smiled. 'Certainly!' she said, echoing her cousin. 'And finding her lair is the first step towards finishing her off for good.'

24

A couple of hours later, after searching almost every backstreet in Holloway, Fin, Eryk and Small finally found a gloomy shop on Crib's Alley with a sign above the door – J. CANARY, APOTHECARY AND DRUGGIST. The shop window was stuffed with syrups and spirits, poisons and purgatives, oils and unguents, all displayed on the shelves in an array of bottles and jars and tins. A handwritten sign was pasted to the dusty pane:

Best leeches for sale

Fin peered in, but both the shop door and the window display were backed with yellowing lace curtains and Fin couldn't make out the inside.

She pulled her cap down over her eyes. 'We can't just stand here,' she said. 'What if Mr Canary comes out and sees us?'

They positioned themselves on the other side of the alley where there was a busy butcher's shop. Propped up outside was a sign in the shape of a pig, which was just the right size to conceal two loitering children and a small dog.

After a while, a woman pushing a pram trudged up to the apothecary's. A bell tinkled as she pushed open the door and went inside. Fin got a fleeting glimpse of the innards of the shop: there was a counter, behind which were shelves stacked with bottles, and on all sides labelled drawers that stretched from floor to ceiling.

Just before the door swung shut again, she caught sight of a splash of yellow in the gloom. *Mr Canary's cravat!* 'See that?' she hissed. 'E's in there. 'E's inside.'

As they watched, the curtains twitched and a hand reached round, took hold of one of the bottles in the window and withdrew again. Shortly after, the woman reappeared, carrying a brown paper package, which she tucked into the bottom of the pram.

Fin sighed. 'We could be here all day.'

Eryk nodded. 'If he visits Countess, he will not go until dark. Maybe we should –'

But just then, Mr Canary himself emerged from the shop and Fin shrank into the shadows. As she watched, he took a large bunch of keys out of his pocket and locked the door, first in the middle, then at the top and the bottom as well. He checked his reflection in the shop window, rearranged his grubby yellow cravat and went off up the alley towards the main road.

'Let us follow,' Eryk said.

Fin grabbed his arm and held him back. 'Hang on a minute – what if the Countess's lair is *inside* Mr Canary's shop?'

Eryk thought for a moment. 'Is possible . . . Must be place that is dark with room for coffin.'

Fin peered up at the building. 'Like an attic? Or a cellar?'

The apothecary's shop was at the end of a terrace, separated from the next row by a narrow alleyway at the side. Fin told Small to stay by the butcher's, and she and Eryk made their way down the alley and skirted round the back. Here, crates stuffed with rubbish were lined up against the buildings alongside the coal hatches. A small sash window in the back wall of the shop was open a crack.

'I'm smallest,' Fin said. 'I'll go first and, if all's well, you follow.'

Together, they dragged one of the crates under the window and Fin climbed up, pushed open the sash and squeezed through. She dropped into a dim room and remained crouched beneath the window, heart thudding, listening for any sign of life. When she was sure there was no one there, she got up and tapped on the glass to let Eryk know the coast was clear.

Fin realized she had climbed into a parlour. There were two armchairs and a side table arranged in front of a cold grate. One of the chairs had a stained antimacassar draped across the back and Fin imagined Mr Canary's greasy head resting there, the oil from his hair lotion seeping into the linen. Fin had lived among filth all her life, but there was something about the place that made her draw in her hands to avoid touching anything.

Between the two armchairs was a small table with a collecting tin on top. Gingerly, she lifted the lid on a dozen squirming leeches. Human-caught, no doubt. She shivered, wondering how familiars fed . . . Did they squeeze the blood out of the leeches or swallow the things whole?

Her thoughts were interrupted when Eryk's head appeared at the open window. He sniffed at the air. 'What is that stink?'

There was the smell of coal dust in the room, and a fainter medicinal aroma, as might be expected in an apothecary's, but underneath that was the pungent tang of blood.

Fin put the top back on the collecting tin. 'It's the leeches probably,' she said.

Eryk had managed to get his head and one arm through the window, but he was both taller and wider than Fin, and she had to help the rest of the way, grabbing hold of him and pulling him until he came through and tumbled on to the rug with a thud.

Fin put a finger to her lips. '*Shh!*'

Eryk got up and dusted himself down. 'I do not fall on purpose.' He glanced around, taking in the cold fireplace, the dusty furniture. 'It look normal, but I do not like this place.'

'I know what you mean,' Fin said. 'Come on.' She went to the door and, opening it a crack, peered through. 'There's no one 'ere.'

They both went through into the shop. Behind the counter, there was another door, this one leading to a staircase. Eryk went to search upstairs while Fin kept a lookout, peeling the curtain back from the window. She could see Small, still sitting patiently on the other side of the road, and she had a good view of the street corner, in case Mr Canary should suddenly reappear.

A few minutes later, Eryk came back down. 'I look in bedrooms and attic. Nothing.'

'What about the cellar then?' suggested Fin. 'There's got to be a trapdoor 'ere somewhere.'

She began searching under the counter. Meanwhile, Eryk inspected the shelves, picking up bottles and sniffing at the liquids inside.

'Nothing,' Fin said after another few moments. 'Maybe it's in the parlour.'

They went through to the back room again. 'Maybe it's under the rug,' Fin said.

Between them, they moved the armchairs and lifted the rug, revealing a trapdoor in the wooden floor. Fin glanced at Eryk.

'This must lead to the coal cellar,' she said hopefully.

Eryk nodded. 'Is perfect place for *strzyga*'s lair, you think?'

Fin took a deep breath. 'Only one way to find out.'

Just as she leaned down to lift the trapdoor, the sound of a key turning in a lock came from the shop front.

''E's back!' Fin's first thought was to get out the same way they'd got in, but it would take too long for Eryk to squeeze back through the small sash window. 'We'll have to put everything back as it was and hide! Quick!'

As they rolled the rug back over the trapdoor and replaced the armchairs, they heard the sound of the second bolt sliding back. In a panic, they looked around for somewhere to hide, but there was nowhere in the parlour so they rushed through to the shop. The third bolt shot back, and Fin and Eryk dived under the counter.

Fin held her breath as the shop door opened with a tinkle of its little bell.

Someone sniffed, and a familiar voice said, 'It stinks of children in here.'

Fin and Eryk glanced at each other in horror. The voice belonged to Dr Hunt.

'It's the customers,' Mr Canary replied with a sigh. 'They *will* insist on bringing their brats in with 'em.'

Footsteps approached across the floor and Fin screwed her eyes shut, expecting to be grabbed by the collar and dragged out from beneath the counter at any moment. But Mr Canary and the doctor went straight through to the parlour, leaving the door ajar.

'Have a seat, Doctor ... Care for some refreshment?'

'Don't mind if I do.'

There was a popping sound, and Fin heaved, realizing it could only be the top being twisted off the collecting tin.

A minute later, Mr Canary continued. 'Now tell me, to what do I owe the . . . *displeasure* of your company, Doctor?'

Dr Hunt cleared his throat. 'I am only here on the Countess's business and I can assure you, Mr Canary, I would not bother darkening your door unless it was absolutely necessary.'

Fin raised an eyebrow at Eryk. The two of them might both work for the Countess, but it was clear from the way they spoke to each other that there was no love lost between them.

'Spit it out then, Doctor. What's the story?'

'That girl you came across – the little redhead. Turns out she's the one the Countess has been looking for all this time.'

Fin's heart thudded in her chest. They were talking about *her*.

'Ha!' Mr Canary replied. 'I knew it, soon as I saw them fingers! Reckon I'll be on page one of the Countess's good books for spotting her.'

'Yes, well,' came the doctor's clipped reply, 'there's been a slight mishap.'

'Oh yes?' There was the sound of someone rubbing their hands together. 'Do tell, Doctor. On your patch, was it, this mishap?'

'It wasn't my fault! I took the Countess to the child's room as usual. How was I to know the girl was hiding under the bed? Apparently, she jumped out just as the mistress was about to feed, and then that Polish boy ran in with a bottle of mandrake . . . and now the pair of them have escaped.'

'I *do* hope, for your sake, that none of that mandrake ended up on the Countess herself?'

There was a long silence, which Mr Canary must have taken as confirmation of disaster. 'Deary me,' he said in mock-concern, 'the Countess must be furious. So where are the brats now?'

'I tracked them down to their aunt's near the Regent's Park. There was a woman there, a Miss Amelia Carmichael, who I managed to lure away, but now the wretched boy and girl have disappeared again.'

Fin and Eryk exchanged a horrified glance. Amelia's telegraphic message from her father had been a fake – Dr Hunt had made the whole thing up!

'So let me get this straight,' Mr Canary said. 'You let them slip through your fingers not once but twice? Oh dear. You can't be very popular . . . I see a chance for a chap such as yours truly to be raised in our mistress's esteem.'

'You snivelling worm!' the doctor spat, all pretence of politeness gone. 'You seem to forget, she's a *countess*. Why would she want anything to do with a low-class druggist like you?'

Now Mr Canary raised his voice: 'An *apothecary*, if you don't mind. Anyway, it's *you* what seems to have forgotten something . . . she's a *strzyga*. You think she cares about who's the most toffee-nosed? No! All she cares about is who can get her that girl. You've had your chance, *Doctor* – it was all handed to you on a plate, but you've managed to mess it up good and proper.'

'Let's get out now,' Fin whispered. 'While they're arguing.'

The two of them crept out from underneath the counter. The old floorboards squeaked and groaned as they tiptoed towards the door, but the quarrel in the back room had grown so heated it covered their escape. By the time Fin and Eryk reached the shop door, the argument had turned into a proper fistfight, and curses and cries of pain emanated from the parlour.

Fin had hold of the door handle and was just opening it when there were several loud thuds from the back room, like the sound of falling furniture, followed by a groan and then silence. In the quiet, there was a tiny *ping* from the bell above the door and Fin froze. She looked up and saw it was poised, tilted back by the door panel. If she moved the door one more inch, it would spring loose again and sound its tinkling alarm, alerting the familiars to their presence. Carefully, carefully, Eryk reached up and covered the bell with his hand while Fin eased the door open the rest of the way . . . then they bolted out of the apothecary's – straight into an enormous belly that was blocking the entire doorway outside.

'Well, well, well,' said a familiar woman's voice. 'Would you look oo's 'ere!'

Fin's heart sank into her stomach. It was Ma Stump, the last person she wanted to see. Snot was with her too, under duress it seemed, since his legs were buckled beneath him and she had him dangling by the collar.

'Fin! What you doin'–?' he managed to squeak, before Ma tightened her stranglehold on him and he fell silent.

With the other hand, Ma reached out and flicked the lapel of Fin's coat. 'Nice togs.'

Fin craned her neck and looked up at her former guardian. 'I were jus' thinking the same,' and she nodded at the new hat Ma was wearing, a wide-brimmed affair with silk ribbons and a stuffed goldfinch perched on the rim. 'S'pose you bought that topper out the cash you got by selling me,' she said.

Ma began a chuckle which turned into a cough, and Fin winced as she was enveloped in a cloud of Ma's navy-rum breath. 'Aww, that's what I like about you, Fin – always quick with the come-back.' She turned to Eryk. 'And who's this ratbag then?'

Eryk drew himself up, affronted. 'My name is –'

'Anyways,' Fin said, interrupting him, 'been nice seein' ya again, Ma, but we must be getting on.' She turned herself sideways and tried to squeeze past.

'Oh no you don't, missy!' And in a single well-oiled movement, Ma thrust Snot through the open doorway, sending him sprawling on Mr Canary's shop floor, while she grabbed Fin and Eryk by their ears, one in each meaty fist.

At the same time, Small appeared from behind the butcher's sign. He rushed Ma, taking her by surprise, and got his jaws round her ankle.

'Argh!' Ma screeched. 'Bleedin' dog! Geroff, you little –!'

She tried to shake him off, but Small dug in and pulled on Ma's leg, forcing her off balance. As she staggered this way and that, she dragged Fin and Eryk to and fro with her, until Fin thought her ear would surely detach itself from the rest of her head. Then Ma recovered and managed to steady herself. Using her free leg, she delivered Small a mighty kick that sent him flying into the gutter on the other side of the street.

A cry rose in Fin's throat, but was squeezed off by the pressure of Ma's fist as she shifted her heavy-duty grip from Fin's ear to her neck. She hauled Fin and Eryk inside, slamming the door behind her so viciously that the little bell flew from its perch and bounced, tinkling frantically, across the floor and into a corner.

'Mr Canary!' Ma bellowed.

The apothecary came rushing out of the parlour into the shop, holding a hand to a bump on his forehead. The doctor limped in after him and stood scowling in the doorway.

'Look what I got!' Ma said triumphantly, thrusting her captives forward.

Fin had experienced Ma's punishment grip many times before and knew the hopelessness of trying to escape, as well as the pain of not staying completely still. But Eryk flailed about, trying to land a punch on his captor. Ma only chortled at his antics and held him at a distance, lifting him off the ground by the ear until he stopped. 'Caught 'em trying to sneak off, I did, and thought you might 'ave something to say about it.'

Mr Canary rubbed his hands together. 'Well done, Ma! This is turning into an excellent day. Bring 'em through,' he said, trying to sweep Ma and her prisoners into the parlour. 'Bring 'em through.'

But Ma didn't budge. 'Not so fast, Mr Canary.'

'Yeah,' Fin choked out. 'Don't do it, Ma. You already got a lovely hat out of it, and I know you ain't really bad, not like these two weasels.'

'Aww, that's nice of you to say so.' Ma shrugged and sighed. 'Thing is, the way I sees it, a chance like this don't come along too often.' She turned back to Mr Canary. 'You get my drift? I have a nose as to the value of these brats, if you take my meaning.'

He hurried over to the till. 'Oh, indeed I do, Ma, indeed I do.'

As the negotiations began, Fin hung her head. All these years she'd stood by Ma, made excuses for her, but now she had to face the truth: Ma wasn't, and never had been, on Fin's side. For Ma, there would only ever be one side – and that was her own. She cared more for her hat, with its moth-eaten goldfinch, than for Fin and Snot.

'Now, what shall we say?' Mr Canary pressed a button and the cash drawer sprang out with an alluring *ping*. 'Twenty pounds for the lot?'

Ma chuckled nastily. 'I might be pickled, but I ain't no muttonhead. An 'undred, or I let 'em run.'

Mr Canary gasped. 'One hundred pounds!' He came out from behind the counter, hands outstretched in entreaty. 'Come now, Ma, I just don't keep that kind of coin in the shop, as I'm sure you'll understand.'

'I understands nothing so well as the flash of gold, Mr Canary,' Ma replied tartly.

The apothecary pawed at his cravat. 'Won't a solemn promise of payment do?'

Ma shook her head. 'It's sovereigns I'm after, not kind words.'

'But Ma, be reasonable. A hundred pounds is an *outrageous* sum.'

'Did I say pounds?' Ma looked around innocently. 'I meant guineas.'

Mr Canary rolled his eyes. 'I've heard that one before.'

On this, Fin found herself agreeing with the apothecary wholeheartedly. It was turning into a nightmarish rerun of the first time Ma had sold her. She could only pray that Mr Canary wouldn't pay up and Ma would have to let them go.

But Fin's hopes were dashed when Dr Hunt, who had been quietly watching the negotiations, suddenly stepped forward and pulled out his wallet with a flourish. 'Do stop quibbling, Canary. Can you imagine our mistress's dismay when I tell her you were *bargaining* over the goods?'

Mr Canary shot his rival a look of pure hatred, but it was clear, as ever, that the wallet had the upper hand.

'Let's pay the woman a fair price and be done with it,' the doctor said, briskly counting a pile of notes on to the counter. A satisfied smirk spread itself across Ma Stump's face.

'Now *that's* what I call a proper gentleman,' she said genially, and she released her charges, grabbed the money off the counter and stuffed it down the front of her dress. 'Nice doin' business with you . . . Mr . . .?'

The doctor forced a smile on to his face and made the smallest bow possible. '*Doctor* Hunt, at your service, madam.'

Ma held out her skirts and gave a clumsy curtsy in reply. 'Well, *Doctor*, here's to a wonderful business arrangement ahead. Trust me, there's plenty more brats where this lot come from,' and she gave him a wink as she stumbled out.

26

Mr Canary hurried to the door and locked it behind her. Then he turned to the doctor with a murderous look. 'I have a few words for you, Hunt, but they will have to wait. Now help me get these three into the cellar.'

The familiars grabbed them and bundled them into the parlour. Neither the apothecary not the doctor had Ma's long experience in the punishment of children, or her vice-like grip, and Fin and Eryk and Snot were able to cause some damage with fists and feet. Nevertheless, after much cursing and thrashing about, the trapdoor was cranked open and they were thrown down a flight of steps into the coal cellar, where they landed in a tangle of arms and legs. The trapdoor banged shut above them and they were left in the dark.

'Fin?' Snot said. 'You all right?'

Fin struggled into a sitting position and rubbed at a sharp pain in her elbow. 'Could be worse,' she said. She looked at Snot's worried face in the gloom. 'Might've hoped for better circumstances, but it's good to see you, Snot.'

Snot's face broke into a grin. 'Bet you missed me, didn't ya?'

'Well,' Fin said, trying not to smile back, 'I didn't miss yer snoring, but –'

A groan came out of the darkness.

'Eryk?' Fin said. 'You all right?'

'I am lucky my ear is still on my head.'

'Yeah, Ma's known for her grip.' Fin winced. 'And her kick.' Her head still rang with the sound of Small's pitiful yelp, and the only thing she could see clearly in the gloom was the image of his little body lying in the gutter. Fin curled her hands into fists. 'She'd better not have hurt him, or I'll . . .'

Eryk reached over and squeezed Fin's hand. 'Small is tough dog. He will be all right.'

Snot narrowed his eyes at Eryk. 'And who's this you're so friendly wiv?'

Despite having just bumped painfully down the stairs, Eryk's reply was as proper as ever. 'My name is Eryk, of family Kaminski.'

'What?' Snot turned back to Fin. 'A bloomin' *foreigner*? You hangin' round with his sort now?'

Fin folded her arms across her chest. 'What "sort" would that be then, Snot?'

'You know what Ma says. Can't trust 'em –' he tapped the side of his head – 'and they're as thick as mince.'

'Shut up, Snot. Eryk saved my life and he's got twice the brains of anyone I know. Anyways, considering what's just 'appened, don't you think it's time you stopped listening to Ma's pearls of wisdom?'

Snot huffed. 'Yeah, s'pose ... Well, nice to meet you then, Eryk,' and he shuffled forward and held out his hand.

Eryk took it. 'You also, Snot ... So, why is Ma bringing you here?'

Snot shrugged. 'To work in the shop, Ma said, only she said the same to George last week, and no one's seen him since.' Snot caught the horrified look that passed between Fin and Eryk. 'What's the matter? What d'you think Mr Canary wants with us?'

Fin drew her breath in through her teeth. 'I don't like to tell you.'

Snot snorted. 'Spit it out, girl. I ain't a baby.'

Between them, Fin and Eryk told him the story of their confrontation with the Countess.

'Nah! You're 'avin' me on,' Snot said.

'I wish we were,' Fin said. 'She only feeds on her own family, though, so you'll probably be all right.'

'Is true,' Eryk said. 'But I hate to say familiars are not so fussy.'

Snot shuddered. 'Why d'you 'ave to tell me that? I ain't never likely to sleep again now –'

There was a crash from above, and the sound of raised voices. Dr Hunt and Mr Canary were arguing again. Fin caught a few of the insults they were trading, but then a door slammed and it went quiet. 'Sounds like they've gone out,' she said.

She looked around the tiny cellar properly. It was low-roofed and gloomy, but a little weak daylight filtered in through a narrow, barred window. Now her eyes had adjusted, she could make out a huge heap of coal stacked against the far wall.

'Well,' Fin said. 'Looks like I was wrong about the Countess's lair being inside Mr Canary's shop.'

Eryk nodded. 'But I think we will soon be finding out where it is, unless we can get out of here before tonight.'

Fin glanced over at the narrow window. Already the light seemed to be fading. No time for talking then – they had to act fast.

'Eryk, you're the biggest,' she said. 'See if you can shift that trapdoor.'

He went up the steps and put his shoulder against it, but it didn't move an inch. Fin and Snot tried the bars at the window, only they were firmly set in mortar and it was the same story there.

'It's no good,' Fin said in dismay. 'We're trapped.'

'I have idea.' Eryk was standing in front of the pile of coal, rubbing his chin. He pointed to the wall. 'You see?'

Fin and Snot came over and stood next to him. 'See what?'

'There is chimney here, behind coal. If we move coal, we can climb out on to roof.'

They set to work straight away, pulling the lumps of coal away from the wall and piling them up against the stairs, which had the added benefit, Eryk pointed out, of making it more difficult for anyone to come down.

As the coal was cleared, a chimney breast with an alcove on either side was revealed. Eryk got down on his knees for a closer look. 'Fireplace has not been used for long time. Is blocked. We need something for scraping.'

They searched the cellar for something they could use. Over by the window, Snot found a rusty nail and some shards of glass from a broken bottle. Eryk wrapped the neck of the bottle in his handkerchief and they took turns using the jagged end to scrape away at the mix of mortar and rubble that filled the fireplace. Soon Fin could feel a breath of cool air coming through the hole they'd made; after an hour, they'd scraped most of the blockage out. She lay on her back, stuck her head into the fireplace and looked up the chimney shaft.

Far above was a tiny circle of light. The way out.

The only way out.

Her heart fluttered as she tried to imagine what it would be like, crawling up into that sooty tunnel, unable to breathe or use her limbs properly in the close space. 'Who's going first?' Fin asked. She could hear Snot breathing loudly through his mouth behind her. 'You all right, Snot?'

There was a tremor in his voice when he replied. 'I said I'd never shimmy up one of them deathtraps again.'

Fin got up and patted him on the shoulder. Being a chimney sweep was the worst job a child could have. Snot's poor lungs had been ruined by it, and she knew all about the climbing boys who had fallen or, worse, got stuck and died in the narrow shafts.

'I will go first,' Eryk said. He got down on his belly and tried to squeeze into the hole, but it was obvious he couldn't fit.

'I am sorry,' he said. 'I am too big.'

Fin nodded in resignation. She took off her boots, tied the laces together and hung them round her neck.

Snot had been leaning against the wall, head down, but now he straightened up. 'I'll be right behind you, Fin.'

'You sure?'

'I ain't going to be no meal for no familiar. Anyways, if you fall, I'll catch ya.'

Snot knelt next to Fin as she prepared to wriggle into the fireplace. 'Remember, it's all about gripping with yer knees, elbows and toes,' he said.

'When you get out,' Eryk said, 'bring back help.'

Fin was so worried about the climb that she hadn't even thought that far ahead. 'Help from who? Aunty Bashka and Amelia won't be back for ages.'

'From police, of course.'

'The police?' Fin's shoulders fell. 'They won't listen to a child, specially not one who sounds like me. Unless . . . there is this one decent bobby we know – Sergeant Malone. Works on our old manor. You know him, don't you, Snot?'

Snot nodded. 'He's a good bloke. I reckon he'll listen.'

Fin looked up the chimney again. 'Well, wish me luck.' She took a few deep breaths and wriggled head first up into the chimney shaft behind the fireplace. It was very narrow and she only just fitted.

As Snot advised, she stuck her knees and elbows out and used them to lever herself up, an inch at a time. It wasn't easy. The walls of the shaft were coated in thick soot, which got dislodged by Fin's squirming, and the clouds of choking coal dust made her cough each time she filled her lungs. It must have been worse for Snot, who, crawling up after her, got all the dust she'd dislodged right on top of his head.

With every movement, the walls tore at Fin's clothes, leaving her elbows and knees exposed for the skin to be scraped off by the coarse brickwork. But she kept going, wriggling and squirming, each time pushing herself a little nearer to the circle of light above her head.

Eventually she was forced to stop and rest. Glancing up, she saw she wasn't so far from the top, but even staying still sapped her strength. To stop herself falling, she had to press her knees and elbows into the walls of the shaft. Her whole body shook with the effort and she knew she couldn't keep it up much longer.

'I can't do it,' she choked out between fits of coughing. 'I ain't gonna make it.'

From far below, Eryk's voice came echoing up the chimney. 'You *can* do it! You are girl with head on fire, remember?'

'He's right. Course you'll make it.' It was Snot, just beneath her. 'Listen, I'm wedged in tight; you can rest yer weight on my shoulders.'

Snot and Eryk's belief in her renewed Fin's confidence. Once she'd rested, she gathered her remaining strength, gritted her teeth and pushed on up. At the top, the shaft narrowed, but after much coughing and wriggling she finally levered herself out of the chimney and emerged, breathless, on to the roof.

She looked back down the shaft. 'Snot?'

He turned his face up to her, so close to the top. 'It's too narrow for me, Fin, but I got that broken bottle in my pocket and with a bit of scraping . . .'

'I'll help you,' Fin said.

'No, someone's got to go and get Sergeant Malone.'

'But –'

'Go!'

'All right, I will. Only first you got to promise me something.'

'What?'

'When this is all over, you won't never go back to Ma's, will you?'

'I dunno . . . I mean, why not?'

'Cos she's proved she don't care about either of us.'

'Course she does. She's Ma. We're practically family. She wasn't to know what that apothecary wanted us for . . . she ain't that bad!'

Practically family. It felt strange to hear Snot use the same argument she herself had used, time and again, to defend Ma. 'No, listen to me, Snot. I used to think that,' she said. 'Even after she sold me to the highest bidder, I kidded myself she done it for my own good. But now I've met people who know what family really means, and I've come to see that Ma only cares about herself.'

She fell silent, expecting Snot to reply, but he said nothing.

'I used to look up to her, same as you,' she continued. 'But I'm done with all that. You and Small were the only ones who ever really cared about me.'

After another lengthy silence, Snot sniffed loudly. 'We ain't got time for this soul-searching now, Fin. Go and get the sergeant, and be quick about it.'

Fin didn't want to leave him, but she knew he was right. With a heavy heart, she turned away and looked across the rooftops. She was in an alien landscape, a world of hills and valleys made of tile and slate, far above the London streets she knew.

Fin clambered from the chimney stack and slid
down the slates into the gulley between the valley
roofs. There, she pulled her boots back on, then ran
up the roof and down again, from one house to the
next until she reached the end of the terrace next to
the main road.

She peered over the edge. There was no easy way
down. The bough of a large plane tree overhung the
roof, but Fin was no tree climber and the branch looked
too thin to take her weight. A downpipe was sticking up
above the roof and she pushed against it to test its
strength. It seemed secure enough, but she felt the pull
of the ground far below and sweat broke out on her
palms and under her arms.

For a moment, she shut her eyes, steeling herself for the ordeal ahead. She thought of Snot and Eryk, who were counting on her. *You can do it*, Eryk had said. Her eyes jumped open again as she realized how much she had come to rely on her cousin and his encouragement. Ma Stump said helping others was a weakness. Fin used to agree with her, but now she knew better.

She glanced up at the sky. Daylight was fading from the horizon, and at the far end of the street, the lamplighter was out with his pole and ladder. Soon the moon would be rising. There was no time to waste.

Just then, she heard a familiar bark and, looking down, saw Small on the pavement at the bottom of the downpipe. Her heart swelled with love for her faithful dog. He must have been outside the shop, waiting for her all this time.

She called to him and, at the sound of her voice, he half-heartedly wagged his tail. Even from up on the roof, Fin could see he'd been injured.

It was all she needed to spur her on. 'Just wait there, Small, I'm coming!' She grabbed the downpipe with both hands and swung her leg round it, clinging to the side of the building, gripping on with feet and knees. *Just don't look down*, she said to herself, as she began the descent. She forced herself to concentrate only on finding the next hand or foot hold and not on Small's injuries or the void that gaped beneath her.

She was almost halfway down when the lamplighter reached her end of the street and caught sight of her. 'Oy! What you doin' up there?' he shouted. 'You a chimney sweep who's got lost?'

Up until then, no one had spotted her, but now a few passers-by stopped to look. They pointed up at her and more people began to assemble to see what was going on. 'Who is she?' they asked each other. 'How on Earth did she get up there?'

The last thing Fin wanted was to create a spectacle. What if Mr Canary and Dr Hunt were alerted by all the commotion?

As Fin neared the ground, the lamplighter positioned his ladder against the wall beneath her, and there was a smattering of applause from the gathered crowd at his quick thinking. Fin stretched a foot down and was able to reach the top rung. At this, there were cheers and the crowd surged forward to clap the lamplighter on the back. 'Well done, man! You've saved her!'

Everyone was expecting a heart-warming end to the drama, an extravagant show of gratitude, or a quick *thank you, sir* at least. But as soon as her feet touched the ground, Fin scooped Small into her arms, dodged round the waiting well-wishers and made off into the dark streets. As she ran away, she heard the indignant complaints of the disappointed crowd behind her. 'Well I never! Would you warrant it? What an ungrateful baggage!'

But Fin didn't care what they thought. 'You're the best dog in the world,' she said to Small as she made her getaway. 'You must be starving hungry, waiting for me all that time.' He was shivering and she held him tight against her to warm him up. 'I'll get you home and fed soon as I can, but first I've got to get the bobbies for Snot and Eryk.'

There were closer police stations, but Fin made for the one on her old patch of Hackney Marsh. If she was lucky, Sergeant Malone would be on duty. At least she knew he would listen to her, when no one else was likely to.

She tore along the streets, dodging the few remaining pedestrians who idled on the pavements. The only thoughts in her mind were of Snot and Eryk, of persuading Sergeant Malone to bash down Mr Canary's door and rescue them from the cellar before the familiars had a chance to bleed them dry. As the dark night drew in, her fears for them grew and she pushed herself on faster.

The shops were closing up now, and her shadow ran alongside her, reflected in the dark windows. She looked a sorry state; her clothes were shredded, her knees and elbows were bloody and scraped of skin, and she was covered from head to foot in coal dust. Even if she'd been clean as a pin, Fin knew that if she asked anyone else for help she'd be dismissed as soon as she opened her mouth. The way she spoke marked her out as a street urchin, and nobody paid any attention to a child, let alone a poor one.

It took nearly an hour to cross town, and by the time she hurtled up the steps of the Hackney Marsh police station, she was desperate. She pushed through the double doors. On the other side, a few bored-looking men were waiting in the entrance, sitting on a bench. Up at the counter, a woman in a turban was holding forth in a strident voice, while the desk sergeant, a bluebottle Fin didn't recognize, was writing down what she said.

Fin rushed up to the counter. 'Where's Sergeant Malone?' she said, fighting for breath. 'I got to see him right now.'

'Oy!' The woman in the turban elbowed Fin out of the way. 'I was 'ere first. Stop pushin' in!'

The desk sergeant looked up from his paperwork. 'Now, now, ladies. No need for that.'

'Please, it's an emergency!' Fin said, forcing her way past the woman to the counter.

'Well, none of us is 'ere for a bloomin' knees-up!' the woman bawled. 'Get in the queue like everyone else, why don't you?' And she gave Fin a shove that sent her sprawling on the floor.

Despite his injuries, Small leaped from Fin's arms and went for the woman. He got hold of the hem of her dress in his teeth and pulled, while the woman tore off her turban and tried to fight him off, swiping at him with the hat. But Small held on, growling and shaking his head from side to side. There was a tearing sound and a long strip of the woman's skirts came away in his mouth.

'Why you little –' The woman backed Small into a corner and reached down to grab hold of him. 'I'll skin ya alive!'

At this, Fin saw red. 'Get away from my dog!' She scrambled to her feet, ran at the woman and pushed her hard. She toppled against the wall, banged her head and let out a howl of rage. The men waiting on the bench had perked up now, delighted by this unexpected distraction. There were shouts of 'Fight, fight, fight!' and 'Knock 'er out, Nelly!'

Nelly clenched her fists and was just gearing up to take their advice when the desk sergeant, who had slipped out at the first sign of trouble, returned with reinforcements. One officer grabbed Nelly and the other grabbed Fin.

28

'Let me go!' Fin shouted. 'I got to see Sergeant Malone! It's a matter of life and death!'

'Oh, I'm sure it is,' the bobby said mildly as he manhandled her away from the front desk.

'But you don't understand,' Fin cried. 'My friends will be murdered an' . . . an' drained of blood!'

Someone on the bench tittered. 'You got a right one there, Officer. She's stark raving mad!'

The bobby chuckled in agreement. He dragged Fin down a corridor, threw her and Small into a cold stinking cell and locked them in. Fin ran to the door. 'Please! It weren't my fault! She started it!'

'You cool off now,' the officer said, 'and we'll see how things are in the morning.'

'But you got to help me!' Fin shouted, kicking the door and beating on it with her fists. But it didn't matter how much she pleaded and cried, the officer left, whistling to himself, and left Fin alone.

Fin carried on screaming and hammering on the door, but no one came. Then she rushed over to the small, barred window in the far wall and shouted for someone – anyone – to help her. But no one could hear.

Eventually, when her throat was hoarse from shouting, she realized it was pointless and she slumped down on to the narrow bed that took up most of the cell. There was no blanket and she curled up with Small, trying to keep him as warm as she could. 'I'm sorry, Small,' she sobbed. 'I've mucked it all up. I've let everybody down.'

Small whined. He snuggled his snout into her neck and licked her face. Her stomach rumbled noisily, but she didn't complain, knowing Small was just as hungry. She thought how he'd gone for Ma and that woman Nelly, how he'd waited for her all that time she was trapped in Mr Canary's coal cellar. He'd been there right at the beginning, protecting her when she was left on Ma Stump's doorstep. Her mother's faithful dog, and now Fin's. She stroked his soft head. 'You're the best dog in the world. If it wasn't for you, I don't know what I'd do.'

Small soon fell into an uneasy sleep, but Fin could not rest. She couldn't stop thinking how she had failed, and what her failure would mean. She thought of Emily, whose body would be drained of blood, her soul eaten up, one memory at a time. She thought of Snot and Eryk, whose hopes of rescue must be dimming with the light. They were at the mercy of the two familiars and, now that darkness had fallen, of the power of the Countess as well.

She thought of the promise she'd made at her mother's tomb, to do her best. She racked her brains, trying to think of what she could do. But there was nothing. Even if she could have got a message out, there was no one to help: Aunty Bashka was miles away at Castle Kaminski and Amelia was just as distant in Surrey.

Then for some reason she thought of Natasha and she sat up. The ghost was frightening, but she too was a victim of the Countess and she clearly wanted to help Fin to defeat her.

Fin shut her eyes and brought the image of Natasha's spectral face to her mind. 'Help me, Natasha,' she whispered. 'There's no one else who can. I'm stuck in jail and Snot and Eryk are in danger.' She waited a moment, then opened one eye, but the cell looked just the same as before and she sensed no other presence in the room.

Maybe she needed to have a séance like they'd done at her aunt's for Mrs Grey? Fin remembered the last thing the ghost had said to her: *Seek me in the mirror*, she'd said. *Find me in the book*.

Well, Fin *had* found her in the *History of the Kaminskis* already. Of course, she didn't have a mirror, but perhaps some other object that reflected an image would do instead? She glanced round the room, but there was nothing. Even the tiny window had no glass in it. She checked her pockets and pulled out her mother's tinderbox.

The only light came from a gas lamp burning in the corridor outside. It sent a few weak rays in through the barred hole in the cell door, but the polished brass lid of the tinderbox captured it and reflected it back at Fin.

She had no table, no candles, no alphabet, and despite the gloom, the cell had none of the carefully curated atmosphere of the Baroness's séance room. But that had all been for show, to impress her gullible customers, and Fin hoped it wouldn't matter here.

She held the tinderbox so that it caught the light. Now, with her own reflection held in its polished lid, Fin tried again.

'Speak to me, Natasha. I need your help.'

This time, a draught of cold air seeped under the door and into the room, making Fin shudder. 'Natasha?' she said. 'Are you there?'

In the tinderbox lid, Fin saw a silvery face materialize out of the darkness. A ghostly six-fingered hand slid over her own, holding it tight in a freezing grip. A shiver took hold of Fin, but she knew the ghost was there to help her, and knowing this she did not feel the terror she had felt before.

'Help me, Natasha,' Fin said. 'Tell me how to defeat the Countess.'

This time, there were no letters for Natasha to spell out her reply. Instead, Fin heard her whispered voice inside her head.

'*You must give yourself up,*' Natasha said. '*You must face the Countess alone.*'

'But I don't know what to do.'

'*The Countess has woven herself a soul from the golden threads of memory she has stolen from her descendants. It is the source of her power and her life. It is her heart. You must destroy it.*'

'What if I fail?'

'*You must not fail. The spirits of all her victims are trapped in the Countess's soul . . . All but one. She murdered me and destroyed my soul, so that I have no peace and can never rest. It was the price she paid to become what she is.*'

'A *strzyga*?'

The image in the reflection nodded. '*After that she fed on memories, and made herself a soul from the threads, so she could live forever.*'

Fin squeezed the cold hand of the ghost. 'Is my mother one of them?'

'*Yes. All your ancestors but me are trapped there, and if you fail, you and every one of your descendants will be imprisoned there too.*'

Fin hung her head. 'You have to tell me,' she said. 'I need to know what happened to my mother, I need to know how she died.'

The ghost did not reply and Fin thought she would never know the answer. But suddenly, Fin's hand was forcibly pressed to her face, covering her eyes and a silent scene began to form in the darkness.

A full moon shone in the sky, its aura so radiant that it bleached the night of stars. It was reflected, in silvery rippling fragments, on the surface of the great moving river that flowed away from the city, beneath Westminster Bridge and back out towards the sea. The bridge was deserted, until the figure of a woman appeared at one end and began to run across. The moon was bright, but her face was hidden by darkness, shadowed by the shawl she had drawn round her head.

She was halfway across when suddenly she stopped. Ahead of her, there was someone else standing on the

bridge. She was dressed entirely in black, and her tall imposing figure seemed to repel the moonlight. It was as if she had no substance and was only the shadow of a person, a silhouette. It was the Countess.

She advanced towards the middle of the bridge, and although the night was still and the gas lamps were encased within glass bowls, their flames flickered and dimmed as her shadowy form passed them by.

The woman turned to run, but now a man approached from the other end of the bridge. She was trapped between them. She staggered to the balustrade and looked over the edge at the dark water churning beneath her.

The Countess raised her six-fingered hand and the woman's head jerked up like a puppet's. Her back arched in pain as she was drawn, one staggering step at a time, away from the edge. The shawl she wore slipped down on to her shoulders and the moonlight etched out the agony on her face as she resisted the power of the *strzyga*. She fought her way back to the balustrade and climbed up on to it. There she stood, facing her attackers, her heels over the edge, so that the slightest touch or breath of wind might have toppled her down into the water below.

The Countess held out her hand and closed it into a fist.

The woman bent over double and coughed up a thread, which shone with its own brightness in the gloom. It was not silver, like the moonlight, but gold.

The Countess reached out her hand for the golden thread, but before she could grab it, the woman stepped back into the empty air.

Her shawl streaming behind her, she fell into the dark depths of the river and was carried away swiftly in its swollen currents.

Now the silent scene faded to total darkness, and Fin found herself once more in the gloomy cell. 'Tell me what to do,' she said. 'And I promise I will destroy her.'

'*Tell her you have seen me tonight and spoken to me. She was human once, and inside her dark heart a small part of that humanity remains. Remind her of what she has done, the memory she can never forget, for even the vilest creature does not want to believe they are truly evil. In this way, you can defeat her.*'

'Remember this,' the ghost said. '*You must not forget a single word. You are the girl with her head on fire, the only one who ever could remember them all.*'

The ghost closed her eyes and began to speak in a low chanting voice, as if she was casting a spell. '*Natasha Lena Kaminski . . .*' she began.

It was the ghost's own name, and at first Fin was puzzled, but as Natasha continued – '*Hanna Nadia*

Kaminski, Henryk Stanislaw Kaminski, Jan Szymon Kaminski, Iza Agata Kaminski . . .' Fin realized she was reciting a list of names.

All of them were members of the Kaminski family. All of them, Fin realized, victims of the Countess. One after another, the names tumbled out. The list went on and on, stretching back to the very beginning of the story, hundreds of years ago. There were so many, but each one stood for a unique person and each one burned itself into Fin's memory.

At last, the list came to an end, the final names being ones Fin already knew: '*Marta Ola Kaminski –*' her own mother, and at the very end, '*Penelope Louisa Worth –*' Emily's sister, the Countess's most recent victim and, Fin promised herself, her last.

When the ghost had finished speaking she bowed her head, and Fin bowed hers too, out of respect for all those souls the Countess had taken.

After a moment, Fin looked up at Natasha. 'It's a list of her victims, ain't it?'

'*Yes, in the order in which they died.*'

'But what's it for?'

'*You have heard of the curse of the Kaminskis?*'

Fin nodded. 'The one I must break?'

'*That is a mistake.*' A rueful smile played on Natasha's face. '*Maria, my nurse, she wrote it down and did not get it quite*

254

right. *The girl with her head on fire must* make *the curse of the Kaminskis. She must make it by naming every one of the Countess's victims.'* Her face hardened. '*I learned the magic from a magician in my mother's court and I have waited such a long time for this.'*

Fin shivered at the ice in Natasha's voice. 'Waited for what?'

'*My revenge.'*

29

Fin woke propped up against the wall, her legs sprawled out in front of her.

'Fin?' Sergeant Malone was standing in the cell doorway with a tin cup and plate.

Fin rubbed her eyes. Had the ghost really been here with her? For a moment she thought it must have been a dream, but she was clutching the brass tinderbox in her hand and the mysterious lilting names Natasha had told her to remember still echoed in her head.

Fin scrambled to her feet. 'Thank goodness you're here!' She rushed over to him. 'No one would listen to me, and Snot and Eryk are in danger! You got to get me out of here!'

'Whoa! One thing at a time. First off, Snot is safe.'

'What? He got out? How?'

Sergeant Malone held out the cup and plate. 'Food first. I got some breakfast and a cup of tea here. And there's an extra sausage for Small an' all.'

'We ain't got time for that –'

'Listen, I'll tell you what happened, but you got to eat some breakfast while I do.'

The sergeant handed Fin the cup and plate and she reluctantly sat down on the edge of the bed. 'So what happened?'

'Well,' he said, sitting down next to her, 'last night the missus and I were woken up by a hammering on the door, and when I answered it, there's Snot standing there, covered head to foot in coal dust –' he nodded towards Fin – 'much like you are. Anyway, he tells me about this Canary fellow and a doctor and what not, and insists I go with him to the apothecary's shop. Claims they've got a Polish boy holed up in the cellar.'

'So you found Eryk? You got him out?'

Sergeant Malone shook his head. ''Fraid not. I made this Mr Canary open up the cellar and searched the house, but there was no one there.'

Fin's hands flew to her face in horror. 'I'm too late then! She's got 'im.'

'She? Who d'you mean?'

Fin thought about telling Sergeant Malone everything, but decided against it. He was a good man and he'd always had time for her, but not even he would believe a story about a centuries-old countess and her blood-sucking familiars. 'Never mind,' she said. 'Just tell me you've arrested him – Mr Canary, I mean.'

'For what? There has to be evidence of a crime for that to happen.'

'Me and Snot were there! We can tell you what happened.'

'I know.' Sergeant Malone looked uncomfortable. 'But that Mr Canary has accused the two of you of thieving –'

'What?' Fin jumped up, sending the cup of tea flying. 'That lying weasel! You don't believe him, do you?'

The sergeant held up his hands. 'Course not. I know you and Snot too well for that . . . but it's his word against yours . . .'

'Say no more. I know how it is – how it always is. No one ever believes kids like us.'

Sergeant Malone could only shrug. No doubt he would have liked to say she was wrong, but he knew as well as anyone there was rarely any justice for the likes of Fin. 'Well then,' he said, 'unless you've got an idea where they've taken this lad, I'm afraid I can't do anything else.'

'There is one thing you can do for me,' Fin said. 'Will you look after Small? Just for a day or two? He's too ill to be dragged around London.'

At the mention of his name, Small opened his eyes and raised his head, but when Sergeant Malone offered him a sausage he only whined and closed his eyes again. 'What's wrong with the little fella?'

'Ma gave him a kicking yesterday,' Fin said. 'He hasn't been right since.'

Sergeant Malone patted Small on the head. 'Poor old chap. He looks done in. I'll take him home with me at the end of my shift. Mrs Malone loves dogs and she's a fine cook – she'll find something to tempt his appetite. She's certainly been feeding that Snot up . . .' He looked thoughtful. 'She's taken quite a shine to the boy, as it happens.'

'I'm glad he's staying with you,' Fin said. 'I made him promise not to go back to Ma's.'

Sergeant Malone nodded. 'He can stay as long as he likes. Now, have you got somewhere to go yourself? You'd be very welcome at ours.'

Fin told him she did have somewhere. She gave him Bashka's address near the park and he wrote it down, as well as Lady Worth's at Castle Kaminski, promising to let her know as soon as he found anything out. 'So where *are* you going now?' he asked her.

'I've got to go down to the river,' she said. 'I need some time to think.'

Sergeant Malone brought her a sponge and a bowl of water, and when she'd cleaned herself up he walked her to the omnibus stop and waved her off.

The bus took Fin south to the river. On the way, she worried about Eryk, where he had been taken and what had happened to him. But there was one thing that gave her hope he was still alive. Natasha's curse had ended with the victim who had died most recently, and last night that had been Penelope, not Eryk.

When she reached the river, she got off and walked the remaining half-mile to the place where her mother had died: Westminster Bridge. She positioned herself in the middle, between two gas lamps, in the exact place her mother had stood.

Fin looked over the parapet. The sun was shining and a sharp breeze whipped up ripples on the surface of the river. This was where her mother had died, where the Countess had murdered her.

In the vision Natasha had shown her, the bridge had been deserted, but now it hummed with carriages and pedestrians crossing in both directions. When her mother fell from the parapet, the river had been high, but now the tide was out and the water level was low. Mudlarks picked over the rubbish the waters had left behind, stranded on the banks, just as they must have done when her mother's drowned body was found, washed up when the tide went out.

The mighty Thames was at its lowest ebb, and Fin felt much the same. One by one, the people she'd come to trust – Emily, Eryk, Bashka, Amelia – they had all been stripped away from her. Now, even Small, her faithful dog, the one who had protected her all this time, was gone. She felt truly alone.

It was all too much to bear and she squeezed her eyes shut, trying to keep the tears at bay. If only she was as brave as Eryk, a proper Kaminski. But she wasn't the person he thought she was. By rotten chance, she'd ended up with Ma, a woman with no sense of right and wrong, who only cared about herself and whose only love was money. Fin had been taught to trust nobody, to look out only for herself. How could she be expected to be any different now?

Fin let her head fall forward into her hands. If she failed, the Countess would wrench her memories from her and Fin would be imprisoned within the threads of her soul. Like Natasha, she would never find any peace or rest.

She looked up as Big Ben chimed one o'clock. The sun was high in the sky, but soon night would come and the Countess's power would grow. Tonight the moon would be full, and the Countess's strength and malice would be complete. Yet the full moon was emblazoned on the family crest, and it had always lent Fin strength. She hoped the Countess was not the only Kaminski who was empowered by its silvery face.

Fin's thoughts returned to Eryk once again. He was in the Countess's power now. If it had been Fin who was in trouble, he would not hesitate to come to her rescue, as he had done before. How could she live with herself if she was not prepared to do the same for him?

For a moment, she considered going back to her old world. Would it be so wrong to run away? To save herself? After all, what chance did she really have against the Countess? Wouldn't she be sacrificing herself for nothing?

But no – she had come too far for that. She didn't want that old life any more. She wanted a new one with the people who had welcomed her and who she now accepted were her true family: Eryk, Bashka, Amelia and Small.

Finally, she turned her mind to her mother. Hadn't she, like Fin, struggled with the very same dilemma? At some point she had realized that her baby daughter was the girl with her head on fire. She had been alone, with no one to turn to, just like Fin. She had left her family without a word, knowing she was ready to sacrifice herself.

In her mind's eye, Fin recalled the image of her mother standing on the parapet, the dark river waters flowing beneath her, the illuminated gas lamps mimicking the full moon in the sky. The Countess had made her mother choke up a memory, and Fin knew it must be the thought of the rickety tenement on the Hackney Marsh, of Ma's doorstep, the place where she had left Fin. Rather than give it up, she had let herself fall. And all so that her daughter could live.

What was Fin's life worth if she didn't use it now to defeat the demon who had blighted her family for hundreds of years?

Fin was heartsick and terrified, but now she knew what she had to do. As Natasha had said, she must go back to Mr Canary's shop and give herself up. There was no middle way. Either she was truly her mother's daughter, or she was Ma's.

For the rest of the day, Fin stood there watching the sunshine play on the water. The boats came and went beneath her, but she hardly noticed, and as evening came on she turned away from the stink of the river and crossed the bridge to the north bank.

She had made her choice. She would honour the promise she made before the statue of the woman and child in her mother's tomb.

'I said I'd do my best for you,' Fin said out loud. 'And I will.'

She told herself she was Magdalena Kaminski, the girl with her head on fire. She would reclaim the memory the Countess had taken from her, and all the other memories she'd stolen. One way or another, whatever it took, she would destroy the demon who had cursed her family and murdered her mother.

She owed it to all the Kaminskis, both the living and the dead.

It was gone seven o'clock and darkness had fallen. The omnibuses had stopped running, and Fin did the return journey on foot. She had no plan beyond knocking on the apothecary's door and demanding directions to the Countess's lair. It wasn't much of a scheme, but she hoped, by the time she got there, that something better would have occurred to her.

As she trudged along, tangled up in her own thoughts, she caught a flitting movement out of the corner of her eye. Fear flashed through Fin's body. She stopped and fixed her gaze on it. The creature was hunched on top of a burning gas lamp, across the street. It was black, and clawed and feathered, but it was not like any bird that Fin had ever seen. It looked back at her with yellowish blinking eyes. Suddenly, it grinned, and Fin saw that it did not have a beak but a mouth full of tiny pointed teeth. The Countess must have sent her familiars out to search the city for Fin, and now she had been found.

As she hurried on, the creature kept pace with her, darting from building to building, not bothering to hide itself. Sometimes it flew ahead and disappeared, only to reappear, lurking in a doorway or crouched at the top of a parapet, high above the street.

As she neared the apothecary's shop, it flew off, and Fin did not see it again until she reached the corner of Crib's Alley. There, just beyond the turning, she spotted a carriage, pulled up at the side of the road ahead. The yellow-eyed creature was perched on top, waiting for her. As Fin drew level, the door of the cab swung open. The interior was in darkness, but a shaft of moonlight shone in and lit up the yellow silk at Mr Canary's throat like a beacon. A moment later, the apothecary's head emerged from the darkness.

'We were beginning to think you weren't coming,' he said, leering at her in a way that revealed his yellow teeth.

We? Fin glanced into the carriage, but apart from the driver and the creature on the roof, Mr Canary was alone.

He put out his hand. 'Why don't you get in?'

Fin stepped back. 'You've gotta be jokin'! I ain't gettin' in there with you.'

'That would be a shame.' The apothecary arranged his face into a semblance of concern. 'Because then, you'd never get to see that young Eryk again. Such a nice boy too, and so full of blood . . .'

The familiar on the roof smacked its lips and Fin shuddered. Her legs buckled at the thought of facing the Countess, but she'd made her choice at the bridge. She would not abandon Eryk or the promise she had made at her mother's tomb.

She took a deep breath, climbed up into the carriage, and sat down as far from the apothecary as she could.

Mr Canary beamed at her. 'The doctor was of the opinion that you'd run away. He said an urchin like you wouldn't have any loyalty, any finer feelings.' He tapped his nose. 'But I knew better. I knew you'd come back.'

'Where is 'e? Where is Doctor Hunt?'

The familiar gave her a ratty grin. '*Unfortunately*, there's been some sort of fuss going on at Castle Kaminski and he had to go back to deal with it.'

Aunty Bashka and Emily! Fin could only hope that they were safe, but forced herself to put that worry from her mind. There was nothing she could do about it now and she must pit all her strength against the danger that lay immediately ahead.

Mr Canary sighed. 'Course, it's left me on me own to deal with you. Not that I mind, since I'll be the one what gets all the glory for bringing you to the Countess.'

'Why do you help her?' Fin said. 'What's in it for you?'

He suddenly lurched forward, a manic look on his face. 'To be near her, and serve her forever.' He raised a hand and tapped lightly on the ceiling, and added, 'Like all those who have shown loyalty to her in their lifetime.'

'What? As one of them flying *rats* she carries around with her? Don't look like much of a life to me.'

'A curious point of view,' he replied, sitting back in his seat with a satisfied smile. 'For someone who has so little of her own life left.'

Fin ignored that. 'So where we going?' she asked.

'Can't you guess?' Mr Canary rubbed his hands together. 'You'll kick yerself when you catch on.'

Fin looked out of the window. The carriage was taking them north, along the same uphill road that she and Eryk had followed the day before. *Of course!* The road that led to Highgate Cemetery.

Fin remembered every detail of her visit to the Kaminski mausoleum – Small's reluctance to enter the grounds, the withered rose bushes in the barren flower beds. It was a place where the Countess could come and go at any hour of the night, and no one would see her. A place, Fin imagined, where a being like the Countess might feel at home.

Mr Canary kept his narrowed eyes fixed on Fin, but did not speak to her for the rest of the journey. The only sounds were the clip of the horses' hooves and, from the roof of the cab, the scratching of the feathered creature's claws.

Now the horses turned into the lane that led to the cemetery gates. The carriage went past the main entrance and drew up further along, opposite a narrow wrought-iron gate.

The apothecary stepped down from the carriage. He spoke to the driver, telling him to wait. Fin climbed out and followed him to the side gate, which opened with a drawn-out creak.

'Please, step inside,' Mr Canary said with a sweeping gesture of his arm, then he stood away from the gateway and made her a mocking bow.

Fin hung back. 'Is Eryk here, with her?'

Mr Canary gave her a jaundiced smile. 'Where else?'

Fin went through the gate and Mr Canary pushed it shut behind her. 'I will leave you here.' He lifted his

chin and sniffed at the air like a dog. 'She knows you are coming. Her followers will escort you the rest of the way.'

Fin turned and began walking along the winding path that led to the Kaminski mausoleum. By day, the cemetery had seemed almost a pleasure park, but the night made the angels with their folded wings seem like demons, and the menagerie of marble animals, which had looked whimsical in daylight, now crouched over their owners' graves, ready to pounce at Fin's approach.

In the far distance, a bank of cloud was rolling in, but here the night was clear. The full moon had risen high in the sky, escaping the clutching branches of the trees. It hung there, lustrous and round, just like the full moon that appeared in the Kaminski book, the same full moon that had lit Fin's vision of her mother's death. Like a brilliant eye, it illuminated Fin's smoky breath in the cold air and picked out the graves, which shone, bone-white in the gloom. It deepened the dark shadows, hiding the living creatures – the foxes, mice and hedgehogs – that crept innocently between the stones.

But the living dead did not hide themselves in the darkness. The Countess's familiars splayed their feathers and bathed in the silvery moonlight. They clustered in the branches of the trees, perched upon the stone crosses and carved statues. They turned their yellow eyes on her and whispered among themselves as she passed them by.

This time, the gates at the entrance to the gardens of the Kaminski tomb were unlocked and when Fin pushed against them they swung open without a murmur. She hesitated and glanced up at the angels who stood on either side, guarding the tomb. One prayed, hands clasped together in repentance, his head bowed in sorrow. The other held a marble sword and shield, his stony face set in anger.

Fin swallowed her fear and steeled herself for what lay ahead. Either she would defeat the Countess, wipe her from existence, or the *strzyga* would live and reign forever. Taking their grief and rage as her armour, she passed between the marble angels and entered the gardens of the mausoleum.

31

Fin climbed the steps, passing between the carved stone columns. For a moment, she stood beneath the marble scroll, engraved with the Kaminski name below the sculpted six-fingered hands.

A trace of the Countess's rotten stink reached Fin on the night air, and with a shrinking heart she stepped through the doorway and peered into the gloom. The darkness that surrounded her seemed to consist of more than just an absence of light. It pressed in on her, forcing the air from her lungs.

She glanced up at the high-vaulted ceiling and stopped dead. A faint glow seeped in through the stained-glass windows, illuminating the dome above her. The dusty hanging swathes of cobweb she'd noticed the day before were transformed by the moonlight. The twisted threads now shone like gold. They splayed out across the dome, tethered to the stony wings of the angels. As Fin gazed up at the web, the shapes within it seemed to come alive, shifting restlessly, like waves at sea. She saw the memory of buildings and landscapes and people, all moving and speaking and living their lives.

It was the web Natasha had spoken of: the heart and soul of the Countess.

A faint sound made Fin turn her head. Something blacker than the darkness crawled across the floor and slipped through the entrance that led to her mother's tomb. Fin's mind went back to the visit she had made to the mausoleum only the day before. She remembered the jagged crack that ran across the top of her mother's stone coffin and, with a flash of anger, she knew that the Countess had broken the seal and made her lair inside with her mother's bones.

Fin crept to the doorway. Beyond it was darker still, but Fin did not need to see to know the Countess was within. The dense reek of decay hung in the damp air, and all around she sensed the flitting movements of the demon's horde. She could hear them, their breath like the purr of many well-fed cats. She strained her eyes, peering into the recesses of the darkness. Now she could make them out, clinging to the statue of the mother and child, bunched like hanging fruit in the corners of the ceiling above her head. Their blinking yellow eyes stared down at her.

There was a breath of movement in the air and an inky mist seeped from the crack in the lid of the tomb. It sank to the ground, swirled and thickened at the foot of the stone casket before it rose and took shape, solidifying into the *strzyga*'s horrifying form. The Countess stepped forward into a shaft of moonlight and Fin saw her face. Although tight and smooth, her skin still bore the scars of the mandrake Eryk had thrown on her.

'Welcome, Magdalena,' she said. 'I knew you could not fail to come.'

There was no echo in that deadening chamber, yet her words were taken up and repeated, spreading among her whispering familiars like ripples on a pond.

'Where is he?' Fin's voice sounded flat and small, crushed by the stifling weight of darkness. But her words too were echoed and grew, buzzing through the gathered swarm: *Where is he? Where is he? Where is he?*

The Countess made a gesture towards the gloomy chamber where stone arches led to each of the other tombs in the mausoleum. 'Come and see.'

She led Fin to the empty chamber where Eryk lay, stretched out on top of the stone plinth, his eyes shut, his body completely still. He was surrounded by the dark fluttering of the Countess's familiars, and Fin's stomach turned at the sharp tang of blood that hung in the air.

'What have you done to 'im?' Fin strained towards him, but she could not step beyond the doorway. 'Is 'e . . .?'

'Dead?' the Countess's lips twitched. 'Not yet . . .' She went over to where Eryk lay and peered down at him. 'To me he is nothing but a maggot on a hook.' She turned to Fin. 'I suppose you imagine you have come to save him?'

'I'm here for her as well.'

'*Her* . . .? You mean your mother?'

'You took 'er from me, and all I had left was a memory – until you stole even that from me too.'

The Countess tilted her head back and looked up at her web, hanging in the moonlit dome. 'Your memory is there with all the rest . . .' The *strzyga* closed her eyes as if savouring the taste. 'A remembered face, the feeling of having once been loved . . . it was not the kind I usually choose to feast upon, yet it had such clarity, such a tantalizing flavour –'

Fin couldn't bear to hear any more. She cut her off. 'I've come to take it back, to take 'em all back. I'm here for all those you destroyed – the ones you murdered just like you murdered my mother.'

The Countess smiled and in every corner of the chamber a multitude of tiny teeth glinted in imitation.

'Murdered? Your mother? No. She chose to die! She threw herself into the river. She could have lived . . . if she had only given me what I wanted.'

'And what was that?'

'The memory of where she left you.' The Countess let out a deep sigh and her fakery was amplified by the goading chuckles of her familiars. 'So sad, wouldn't you say? To have sacrificed her life for nothing?'

Fin fought the urge to cry. 'It weren't for nothing. She did it to save me.'

'Save you? How so? You're here now, aren't you?' The Countess shook her head in wonderment. 'It could not have been more perfectly arranged. Tonight of all nights, when the cold moon is full in the sky. And you, still a child, bursting with a lifetime of the most delicious recollections, a feast of perfect memories that only the girl with her head on fire could give me. Once I have added them to my web, I will be truly young again, I will be immortal, unstoppable. My gratification has only been delayed, and it will be all the sweeter for the wait.' Her voice remained cool, but the familiars expressed her mounting excitement, chuckling and smacking their lips in delight.

'I admit she hid you well,' the Countess continued. 'Who would suspect a mother would leave her only child to the care of strangers, to a life mired in poverty and hunger? Yet it was all for nothing. No one can escape destiny, and your end would have been the same whatever she did.' She arranged her face into an expression of false regret. 'If only she could have seen the future. It would have been far kinder to let you enjoy your short life with a loving family, rather than condemn you to the mean existence you had to endure.'

The Countess's tormenting words made Fin's anger flare up. It raged through her blood like a firestorm and burned her fear away.

'What do *you* know of a mother's love for her child?' Fin retorted. 'My mother did what any mother would've done . . . but someone like you couldn't begin to understand that.'

The Countess did not reply, but her minions muttered angrily among themselves and Fin remembered what Natasha had said about the memory the Countess could never forget. *Even the vilest creature does not want to believe they are truly evil.*

Fin pushed on. 'After all, what kind of mother puts her own life before her child's?'

The Countess narrowed her eyes. 'I expect you got that story from that so-called history book. You shouldn't believe what it says. It is full of lies.'

'No, you can't face the truth. Only a monster would sacrifice her own daughter —'

'Enough! You don't know what happened. You know nothing of my daughter!'

'Oh, but I do,' Fin said. 'I've seen her –'

'That cannot be.' The Countess dismissed Fin with a wave of her hand, but there was no hiding the note of uncertainty in her voice. 'She is long dead and buried far away.'

'I've spoken to her.'

This time, the Countess could not hide the fear in her eyes. 'When?'

'Last night.'

Now, even the horde stopped their muttering and fell silent. A look of dread came over the Countess's face, but she covered it with a careless laugh. 'And what did she say?'

'That she suffers. They *all* do. All of your victims. None of 'em can find any peace, not even in the grave. Not while you continue to live. She's the one who told me what to do, who helped me find you –'

'Helped you? How? By leading you here?' The Countess's face cracked open in a triumphant smile. 'Then where is she now?' She pretended to search for her, looking into the corners of the room, and her minions screeched with laughter. 'Don't tell me she's abandoned you?' the Countess went on in mock concern. 'They all do that, don't they? First your mother, the

279

cruellest cut of all, and then the boy. And now even a ghost can't be bothered to turn up, although one would think she had nothing left to lose.'

The demon took a step towards her, and although Fin would have done anything to step away, to escape the sickening stench of her presence, she found herself helpless, rooted to the spot. 'Do you see now? Do you understand? They have all left you to face me alone.'

Fin wanted to say that the Countess was wrong, that none of them had wanted to leave her. But she had never felt so alone and helpless, and all her hopes melted away under the demon's searing gaze. Fin had done everything Natasha had told her to do. She had reminded the Countess of what she had done, she had told the *strzyga* she had spoken to the ghost of her murdered daughter, and at first it had seemed to be working. But now she understood it was all for nothing. The Countess was too powerful. Fin had failed.

'You will tell me all your stories, both good and bad,' the Countess said hungrily. 'You will leave nothing out, not a single detail. You will tell me everything.' She leaned towards her and Fin found that she could not pull back. 'The first memory I shall take will be last night's. If my daughter really has risen from the grave, I will see it for myself.'

The Countess held out her six-fingered hand.

Fin felt a tearing pain inside her. She tried to resist, but it was no use. Her words choked out of her, coughed up as a shining length of golden thread.

The familiars let out a gleeful cry as their mistress took hold of the shining thread and teased it out, winding it round and round her fingers. Fin spoke of the day before, the visit to her mother's grave, of finding the apothecary's shop, her imprisonment in the cellar and her dreadful scrabbling escape up the chimney. As Fin's recollections poured out, the Countess's appearance began to change. The scars on her skin faded and a new and unblemished face emerged, a face that for all the world was beautiful, even though its beauty was no more than skin-deep.

The full moon shone in on the Countess, gilding her triumphant smile as she drank in the words that Fin could not help but speak out. Her memories were wrenched from her. With every word, she felt her strength ebb away.

The Countess called her familiars to her and handed them the coil of golden thread. They flew with it, up into the vaulted ceiling where the *strzyga*'s soul gleamed golden in the moonlight. They perched on the wings of the angels and flitted back and forth, passing the thread between them, weaving Fin's spirit into the glistening web.

Now Fin spoke of her flight across London to find Sergeant Malone. She swayed with exhaustion as she told how her face and clothes were covered in coal dust, how she ran with Small pressed close against her. The Countess seemed to linger on the memory of her desperation, to draw energy from it. She smiled as Fin's voice cracked and she fell to her knees, as she told of being thrown into the cells, crying out for help, beating her fists against the iron door.

But then the Countess's eyes widened and the smile slid from her face. Fin had reached the moment in her story when she held her mother's shining tinderbox and called on Natasha for help, the moment when the ghost's icy six-fingered hand had taken hold of her own. The

Countess stopped teasing out the golden thread and twisting it round her fingers. Fin fell silent and the tearing pain inside her head began to fade away.

'Natasha?' the Countess looked fearfully around her. 'Is it you? Are you here?'

There was no reply, but the Countess began to gasp for breath.

At this, Fin raised her head.

Now she understood what she had to do. She gathered all the strength that was left to her and cast her flawless memory back to the curse she'd learned that night in the prison cell. '*Natasha Lena Kaminski,*' she began.

Fin's voice was hardly more than a whisper, but at the mention of her daughter's name the demon shuddered, and although she fought against it, she choked up the name herself: '*Natasha Lena Kaminski . . .*'

At this, Fin felt her strength returning and she staggered to her feet. '*Hanna Nadia Kaminski –*' she said, her voice a little louder this time. '*Henryk Stanislaw Kaminski, Jan Szymon Kaminski, Iza Agata Kaminski . . .*'

The Countess put one hand to her throat, the other over her mouth. Now it was not Fin who was forced to speak, but the Countess. She tried to stop herself, but could not help choking out the stream of chanted names, the same names that the ghost had made Fin remember the night before.

Natasha's curse, her revenge.

And as Fin continued, the air around her fizzed and the golden thread crackled with the power of the mounting curse.

The Countess backed away. She tried to break the golden thread, to unravel it from her fingers. But the thread remained taut and strong, joining Fin to the Countess's stolen soul. Through it, Fin could feel the demon's growing sense of dread as together they recited the names of every one of her victims . . . *Aleksander Jacub Kaminski, Dorothea Adela Kaminski . . .*

The horde of familiars could not help but echo their mistress. They too took up the chant, repeating it from the dark corners of the tomb. As Fin spat out the final names – '*Marta Ola Kaminski, Penelope Louisa Worth*', her mother's and Penelope's – the sound grew. It rose up, and was amplified to a roaring wave in the soaring vaulted ceiling above Fin's head.

The roar faded and the shining thread between Fin and the Countess snapped in two. It fell to the floor, where it lay on the cold grey stone like nothing more than a wisp of broken spider's web.

In the silence that followed, the Countess held her hand up in front of her face. She let out a cry at the sight of her flaking fingernails, the liver spots, the veins that pushed up, blue and twisted, from skin that sagged from her bones.

Fin watched in horror as the demon lurched forward in agony. Her familiars flew to her. They purred and cooed, they rubbed their furred and feathered bodies against her. But they could not comfort her, or stop the change that Fin's curse had begun. The chanted names took back the Countess's stolen youth, chiselling deep lines on what had once been her beautiful face.

As the Countess's transformation continued, Fin felt in her pocket for the tinderbox. She drew it out and held it so that her face was reflected in the shining lid. 'Natasha!' she cried.

At once she saw another shimmering face alongside her own and felt an icy hand slip over hers. Fin turned to see the ghost standing next to her.

'Quickly!' Natasha said. 'Unravel the web and you will set the Countess's victims free.'

Fin reached down for the thread that lay on the floor and began to wind it round her fingers, taking back the memories the Countess had stolen.

The Countess lifted her greying head and saw her daughter standing beside Fin. 'You!' she cried, and the familiars let out an angry hiss as they swarmed round their mistress.

'Yes, here I am,' Natasha replied.

'You cannot stop me now. Stand aside!' the Countess demanded.

Natasha stepped between the demon and Fin. 'You shall not pass. I will destroy you, as you gladly destroyed me.'

The Countess's conviction seemed to falter. Just for a moment, the monstrous truth of what she'd done settled on her ravaged face. But it could not take hold. 'No,' she said. 'That isn't how it happened. I never meant for it to end the way it did.'

'Then what did you mean?'

'I only wanted to live, to be young and beautiful again. Is that so wrong?' She shook her head. 'I had no choice!'

'There is always a choice,' Natasha said. 'Each time you chose the bad, the next time it was worse, until you no longer knew the difference between good and evil and you were lost.'

All the Countess's and her familiars' attention had been on Natasha, but now the demon was ageing fast and her back bent with a crack. She looked past the ghost of her daughter and her gaze came to rest on Fin.

'Get out of my way!' the Countess screamed. 'I will not let her destroy my beautiful heart.'

She sent her familiars surging forward. They flew at Natasha, and she fought back, but there were so many of them. They swarmed over her and the phantom was forced back.

Desperately, Fin wrenched the threads from the web and wound them on to her fingers. As the thread unravelled, she saw and heard and felt the memories of the Countess's many victims. There were snatches of sounds and music, of thoughts and words that were foreign to Fin. But there were also people and places she knew: she saw little Emily playing in the gardens of Castle Kaminski with an older girl. *Penelope.*

The whispering ghosts of all those who had died now gave their stories to Fin. Out of this multitude a single tale emerged: the story of a family who had pitted themselves against an evil ancestor, who had battled to destroy her, to free themselves and their descendants and redeem their family name. But the story lacked an ending; the Kaminskis had, so far, failed.

Fin glanced up and saw the many ghostly figures entangled in the weave. They writhed and fought to escape the binding golden yarn. As they struggled free, the web no longer gleamed like gold. The broken threads they left behind hung limp and lifeless.

One by one, the ghostly figures emerged. They looked down at Fin from the vaulted ceiling and whispered among themselves. 'She has come at last and freed us,' they said, 'the girl with her head on fire.'

They seemed to want to stay and fight, but one after another they faded and disappeared into the night.

From outside the mausoleum, there came a distant roll of thunder, and above Fin's head another spirit worked itself free of the web. This apparition did not fade and disappear like the rest, but flew down and came to stand beside Fin. She brought with her the sound of falling rain, and her face streamed with rivulets of water. They ran out of her sodden hair, down over her eyelids and cheeks. They dripped from the soaking shawl she held round her shoulders.

'Magdalena,' the spirit said, and her voice set off a tingling shiver in Fin. It was not a memory exactly, more like the echo of a memory she had once had. Fin had a feeling that once she had known her and been held in her warm safe arms. She realized the dripping spectre must be the ghost of her drowned mother.

'Hurry,' the ghost said, urging her on.

With every wind of the thread, Fin could see the Countess ageing, weakening. But Natasha was weakening too, and she was losing the battle with the familiars.

Marta's spirit turned to Fin. 'The tinderbox,' she said.

The *History of the Kaminskis* flashed before Fin's eyes, the illuminated image of the girl, surrounded by fire, and Eryk's voice in her head . . . *Girl with head on fire must burn heart of* strzyga. *It is the only way.*

Fin gazed at her own reflection in the shining brass lid, her long hair, wild and red as fire. For a second, she hesitated. She knew what burning the web would mean: the memories that still lived in the weave would be consumed, and Fin's own lost memory of her mother would turn to ashes and be lost forever.

Fin felt the icy dripping touch of her mother's hand against her cheek. 'Yes, your memory of that love will burn, but neither fire nor water can ever destroy love itself.'

Fin opened the tinderbox. She thrust her fingers into the steel and smashed it against the flint. A shower of sparks flew out and landed on the ragged dangling threads, where they took hold.

The lifeless weave was tinder-dry, and the fire caught easily and grew and spread. The flames ran up the broken threads towards the web that hung between the columns of the mausoleum, tethered on the soaring wings of the angels. The fire travelled onwards, burning as it went, until it reached the middle of the web that still glimmered with golden light.

As the living threads at the heart of the web flared up, the Countess and her minions shrieked in fury. The last of the demon's stolen youth was burned from her face and body, shrivelling away from the rotten decay that had always lain hidden underneath.

The familiars made a last desperate attempt to reach Fin. They pushed Natasha back, forcing her into the trailing burning threads and she caught alight herself. Some familiars burned up with her, others streamed away, returning to their mistress's side as Natasha's ghostly body was consumed by the flames. But Natasha had already died once, and although her ghostly body burned, she could not die again.

The Countess regarded her own crumbling body with horror. 'Do not leave me like this!' she cried out to her daughter.

And Natasha opened her flaming arms to her mother. 'Come to me then,' she said.

Through thick swirling smoke, Fin saw the look of resignation on the Countess's withered face. As her skin cracked and peeled away, she knew that her long life was over, that she had lost. She stumbled forward into her daughter's fiery embrace, and as the flames torched the two of them, they twisted together in a mockery of dance, a parody of love.

The familiars who still lived leaped into the inferno and burned up with them, until eventually all that remained was a spreading pool of vapour, boiling blue and white on the stony floor of the mausoleum.

The *strzyga* was destroyed, but in the dome above, the web still burned and wisps of crackling thread began to spiral down.

The ghost of Fin's mother turned to her. 'Quickly!' she cried. 'You must get out!'

'I won't leave without Eryk!' But as Fin started towards the tomb where he lay, a piece of the burning web fell into the doorway, barring the way through.

At the same time, there was a splintering sound above their heads, and Fin looked up to see one of the stone angels toppling from the vaulted ceiling. It plunged head first to the floor and smashed to pieces in the entrance of the mausoleum. With it, huge swathes of the burning web came untethered, and fell down around it, blocking the way out behind a wall of fire.

Marta's ghost took Fin's hand. 'Come, or it will be too late.'

Fin pulled away. 'Not without Eryk!' She rushed to the tomb where he lay and stamped out the burning web that blocked the doorway.

Once through, she ran to him. 'Eryk!' she shouted, shaking him. She wrapped his arm round her shoulders and pulled, but he was a dead weight. 'Wake up! I can't move you, you're too heavy.'

Only then she felt her mother's ghost beside her, and suddenly she had the strength to lift Eryk from the stone coffin where he lay. She dragged him to the doorway and out into the vaulted chamber of the mausoleum.

All around them, pieces of the burning web rained down. One fell on Fin and caught a strand of her hair alight. She felt it blaze up, as fast as tinder, but her mother was still with her and she opened her dripping arms. 'Come to me,' the ghost said.

It was an echo of what Natasha had said and, just as the Countess had done, Fin stepped into the ghost's embrace, dragging Eryk with her. Together, they carried him, clambering over the fallen angel that blocked the way out. Together they stumbled into the wall of flame.

Only this was no parody of love. Fin's mother had willingly given her life for her, and the agony of her drowning was repaid. The filthy Thames water that had filled her lungs and choked her life away now held off the flames that surrounded them. They fought their way through and emerged, unscathed, into the safety of the garden beyond, where a fine rain was now falling.

They laid Eryk down on the ground, beyond the reach of the leaping flames, and Fin collapsed next to him, choking in the smoke-filled air.

Together, they watched the mausoleum burn. The stained-glass windows exploded in the heat. Towering flames leaped out and smoke poured from the blackened holes they left. With a sound like a crack of thunder, the domed roof collapsed and fell in on itself, releasing plumes of flame and dust and smoke.

Fin reached up and took hold of her mother's dripping six-fingered hand. 'Everyone said you'd abandoned me forever,' she said. 'But I always knew you'd come back.'

The ghost crouched down and took Fin's face between her icy hands. She stroked away the soaked and blackened strands of hair that were plastered against her cheeks. But then she flinched, as if at a distant sound, and got to her feet. She looked over her shoulder, away from the burning mausoleum, towards the wild woods that surrounded them. 'They are calling me,' she said.

Fin could see her mother was fading, that the hand she held was slipping from her grasp. 'Please . . .' she said, 'don't go.'

The ghost looked down at her and smiled sadly. 'I cannot stay . . . but you will remember me, won't you?'

Fin clutched her mother's hand more tightly, but it dissolved into the night, and Fin was left with nothing but her tears and the sound of falling rain.

THE DAILY HERALD

24th November, 1866

MYSTERIOUS CASES OF
SPONTANEOUS COMBUSTION

London police were puzzled by the discovery last week of the burned bodies of two men. One of the deceased has been named as Josiah Canary, apothecary, whose body was found in the parlour of his shop in Holloway. The other was identified as Wilfred Hunt, whose lifeless body was found in the guest suite of Castle Kaminski in Essex.

The bodies of both men had been almost completely consumed by fire, yet there appears no obvious motive for their deaths, and, remarkably, in each case no match or other combustible material to cause the blaze was discovered, nor was anything else in the rooms where they were found damaged by flame.

During their investigations, detectives discovered that Wilfred Hunt had fraudulently taken the title of 'Doctor' and had been posing as a medical practitioner, despite having no medical or other suitable academic qualifications. Curiously, the two gentlemen seem to have known each other, although this link has not led police any closer to the truth of what happened.

Yesterday, a verdict of misadventure was recorded by the coroner. Police have closed the case and are not seeking anyone in connection with any crime.

Epilogue

Castle Kaminski, four weeks later

It was a beautiful winter's day, crisp and cold, and the sun gilded the mists that rose off the marshes. Fin, Small and Eryk sat opposite Bashka and Amelia in a hired carriage, on their way to Castle Kaminski.

Following the fire at the mausoleum, Eryk had been sick in bed for weeks. Amelia had been inconsolable, saying she should have realized the telegraph message was a forgery and blaming herself for leaving Fin and Eryk alone and unprotected. Bashka and Fin had done everything they could to comfort her, to convince her that none of what had happened had been her fault. But she remained quiet and downcast, until the morning when Eryk sat up in bed and demanded a huge breakfast, and it was clear he was on the mend.

Now Eryk was completely well again, Amelia was back to her old cheerful self, and they were all excited to be on their first trip out.

On the way, they'd stopped off in Hackney to visit Snot. When they'd arrived, Small was first out of the carriage and had leaped into Mrs Malone's arms. She was a woman who expressed her love through food, and Small had developed an unbreakable attachment to her as she nursed the little Jack Russell back to strength with huge bowlfuls of her famous Irish stew and dumplings. It seemed to have worked on Snot too – Fin hardly recognized the boy who looked so happy and had put on so much weight.

'He's got a wonderful appetite,' Mrs Malone had agreed, ruffling Snot's hair. 'He can stay as long as he likes, provided he attends school and gives up the apple scrumping.'

Now, as Castle Kaminski came into view, Small stood on Fin's lap and, planting his feet on the windowsill, gave an excited *wuff*.

Fin herself was nervous. She might have been born at the castle, but she had decided she would never come back here to live. She knew it wasn't a place where she would ever truly fit – besides, she was happy in London with her unusual but loving family. Fin was adamant she should earn her keep, and Bashka had said she and Eryk could help with the séances and had put them in charge of spooky noises and ectoplasm.

As the carriage drew up in front of the house, Mrs Benton came out to greet them. 'I'm afraid Lady Worth is indisposed,' she said. 'But Miss Emily will be delighted to receive you.'

The housekeeper led them to the drawing room where Emily was lying in front of the fire on a *chaise longue* with a blanket over her knees. She still looked frail, but there was colour in her cheeks, and when the party were shown in she got up and hugged each of them in turn.

They had tea, and as it was almost Christmas, Aunty Bashka handed out presents while Eryk told Emily about their plans for the following summer. 'Amelia is arranging a mountaineering expedition to Poland. We are all going, and you can come too,' he said excitedly.

Emily smiled. 'I'm not sure Mama will like it, but my new doctor says fresh air is the best cure.' She leaned towards Fin and whispered, 'He says bleeding is the worst, and won't even allow leeches in the house.'

After tea, everyone had eaten so many cucumber sandwiches and so much cake that Amelia insisted they go out on the marshes and walk it off, but Fin stayed behind with Emily.

'You know,' Emily said when they were alone, 'I still have nightmares about that woman. And as for what happened to that terrible man, Doctor Hunt –'

Fin took her hand. 'You're safe now. The Countess and all her familiars are gone forever.' She went on to tell Emily all the things that had happened since she and Eryk had run away from Castle Kaminski. She told her about Natasha showing her the vision of her mother's death, and how the ghost had cleverly laid a trap for the Countess by embedding her curse in Fin's mind; and she described how her mother's ghost had been freed from the web of memories and had saved Fin and Eryk from the fire.

'Were you very much hurt?' Emily asked.

'Not much – look,' and Fin pulled off her cap, revealing half an inch of new-grown fiery hair.

'What about the memory of your mother?' Emily asked. 'Did you get it back?'

'No, but it's all right. I got a new memory of her now, and I'll never forget what she did for me – what she did for all the Kaminskis.'

'None of us will. But . . .' Emily bowed her head.

'But what?'

'I feel so sad about the memories I have lost, especially the ones of my sister Penelope. I don't remember her at all.'

Fin nodded. 'I understand.' After a minute she reached into her pocket. 'Look, I got something for you.' She took out the present she'd brought for Emily and handed it to her.

'Thank you! How lovely,' Emily said. 'I shall look forward to opening it at Christmas.'

'Open it now,' Fin said.

So Emily took off the wrapping paper. 'Oh, it's a book!' She looked at Fin. 'You wrote this yourself?'

'Amelia's been teaching me. She makes it look easy, but it's much harder than reading, and every time I put that pen on the paper the ink goes all over the place and I end up with a horrible mess. But all them stories and memories I saw in the Countess's web can't be lost. They have to be recorded, and like Amelia keeps reminding me, that means writing 'em down.'

Emily leaned towards her. 'Did you . . . did you see any of *my* memories?'

'I did.' Fin took the book from her and read the pages where she had written, in spidery purple ink, the memory she had witnessed in the mausoleum: the story of two fond sisters, Emily and Penelope, who, on a sunny summer afternoon, had played with their dolls in the garden, and drunk cold tea out of tiny china cups and been perfectly happy.

Emily sobbed as Fin read, but when she finished she took the book back and pressed it to her heart. 'Thank you. It's the best present anyone could ever give me.' She opened the cover and read the title in the flyleaf:

The History of the Kaminskis
Part Two
by Magdalena Kaminski

She looked up at Fin. 'So you have accepted who you are at last?'

'Oh yes, I'm a Kaminski all right,' she said. She linked her extra pinky to Emily's, in the family greeting that Eryk had taught her that night on the marshes. 'But you can call me Fin.'

ACKNOWLEDGEMENTS

The idea for this story came from a fairy tale I wrote ten years ago, about a demon who steals the stories of children and weaves them into a tapestry in order to live forever. I was searching for a new idea and had been reading about unusual jobs and came across leeching. The two ideas merged in my mind, along with a bit of Polish mythology and a hint of *Oliver Twist*, to create the story of *Fin and the Memory Curse*.

My thanks go to all the people who helped me with this book, which was written during lockdown:

To brilliant Jo Williamson, the best and wisest agent a children's author could hope for.

To my amazing editor, Emma Jones. A kind of magic happens when I work with Emma, and as it did with *The Ice Whisperers* – she helped me uncover and deepen the heart of the story, which is the story I most want to tell.

To super-creative illustrator, Marco Guadalupi, who has again created a gorgeous cover and beautiful illustrations that bring Fin's world to life.

To all the talented people in the Puffin team, who know exactly how to polish, present and promote a story and make it shine.

To my inspirational Bath Spa University tutors, Steve Voake and Julia Green, who enabled me, and so many others, to develop the skills and confidence to write for children.

To my wonderful, supportive writing group – Lu Hersey, Eugene Lambert, Kim Lloyd, Nicola Lush and Val Mote – who encouraged me and helped me hone the first draft over Zoom and email.

To Salt and Sage Books for such a positive and educational sensitivity read.

To my son Joe and stepson Leon, and to my lovely friends, Alli, Anna, David, Lucy and Ray, and with special thanks to Sally Gamble, for lending me her name, and Laura who read an early draft and pronounced it 'a page-turner'.

Lots of people have supported me with my writing, but no one more than my husband Kat, my first reader and critical friend.

Finally, to Mum, who is greatly missed, and who taught me to read and love books.

ABOUT THE AUTHOR

Helenka Stachera grew up in a yellow-brick house in the woods with her British mother and Polish father, which stoked her lifelong obsession with fairy tales and legends. In her magical novel, *Fin and the Memory Curse,* she continues to explore themes of family and belonging that, as an adopted daughter, are very close to her heart. Helenka lives with her husband and many houseplants in Bristol.

Praise for *The Ice Whisperers*

'An enchanting debut'
Sophie Kirtley, author of *The Wild Way Home*

'Full of magic and adventure'
Radiya Hafiza, author of *Rumaysa: A Fairytale*

'An engrossing read' *The Scotsman*

PROLOGUE

Northern Siberia, 40,000 years ago

The wind changes direction, veering from the west to the north. Ren-*ya* lifts her face to the breeze and sticks her tongue out into the drifting snow. She tastes pine resin, the mineral tang of ice, the day-old musk of elk. But something else is carried to her on the wind from far away, something that burns the back of her throat. She recognizes the faint, sharp flavour: *white-eyes*.

Ren-*ya* follows the flavour upwind. Her snowshoes make her fly and she hardly leaves a mark as she runs over the deep white drifts. She positions herself at the top of a ridge. Crouched behind a stand of gnarled spruce trees, she waits. The morning passes and at last the invaders appear: hunched figures emerging from a

ghostly mist. Ren-*ya* watches from her hiding place as they approach, counts them as they pass beneath her. Ten shrouded warriors lead the way, their heads feathered under their hoods. Then come the followers, strung out in a line behind them, walking in twos. Each pair hefts long wooden poles between them that creak with the weight of bison hides, water sacs, the dangling limbs of a recent kill. They slog on, heads bowed.

From time to time, one of them looks up and she catches sight of their eyes. They are milk-white, and, in the centre, each has a darting circle that is brown or grey, sometimes blue. So different to the wide black eyes of Ren-*ya*'s people, the Last.

Animals travel with the *white-eyes*. They look something like wolves, only they lick the humans' hands and trot at their heels as no wolf

ever would. One draws level with Ren-*ya*, no more than twenty strides away. It lifts its blunt snout and snuffs at the air, but Ren-*ya* has deadened her odour with juniper and not even a cave bear could sniff her out.

She follows them all day and in the late afternoon, when the sun skims the tops of the trees, they stop and make camp. Ren-*ya* watches as they gather firewood, erect the wooden poles and cover them with the bison skins. She listens to their chatter, although she cannot understand the sounds they make. They are as alien to her as their animals are to wolves, yet she has heard them laugh and even sing. She is both fascinated and afraid. Part of her would like to step out, show herself, but, although Ren-*ya* is not yet grown, she knows they would skewer her before she had a chance to raise her empty hand in peace.

As darkness falls, she slips away and runs through the night.

She is still some way from home when she sees her mother, Nagar, coming towards her in the creeping light of dawn. Ren-*ya* runs and throws her arms round her, too breathless to even say her mother's name.

'Where have you been?' Nagar says. Then, when she sees Ren-*ya*'s face, 'What has happened?'

'*White-eyes.*'

Her mother presses her hand to her heart and calls on the ancestors for help. 'Come,' she says. 'We must tell Hebera at once.'

They hurry over the mounting snowdrifts and run through forest trees hung with ice, every breath blooming in the air like a puff of smoke. Eventually, they cross the wide, frozen river and reach the caves. At the entrance, Ren-*ya* blows the horn and the Last troop out of the dark tunnels and sit round the meeting fire. They wait in silence for their leader, the shaman Hebera.

She emerges from the caves, an old woman with a face so still and set it might be hewn from rock. A black-feathered bird sits on her shoulder and she wears the splayed wings of a vulture for a cloak.

'What news, Ren-*ya*?' Hebera says.

'The *white-eyes* are coming.'

'How far?'

'A night of running.'

Ren-*ya* can taste the sour-milk flavour of fear that seeps from the skin of her people. A generation has gone by since the *white-eyes* first appeared on the plains. Back then, the Last sent a handful of warriors to welcome them. They took gifts of meat and berries, the tail feathers of hawks, the carved canines of a sabretooth. But none of those who went to meet the *white-eyes* were ever seen again. Every year, the invaders push further north. The Last have fallen back into the snowy forests, retreated to the very edge of their world. Now there is nowhere left to run.

'How many?' Hebera asks.

'More than fifty,' Ren-*ya* says. 'They have no infants with them, no old.'

Hebera drops her chin to her chest. 'Then they are here for war.'

The great warrior, Malor, stands up. 'We must fight!' He is taller than Hebera and he looks over her head to meet the eyes of his people. 'We are better than them, stronger, faster. I will lead our warriors to war.'

'Even if you defeat them,' Hebera says, 'do you think no more will come? We are the Last. We have fewer than thirty warriors. If we die, no more like us will ever live.'

Suddenly a log in the fire explodes, spitting out a burning ember that lands at Nagar's feet.

'The spirits would speak with us, Nagar,' Hebera says. 'Eagle, Raven and Crow will tell us what to do.'

Hebera orders a great fire to be built in the spirit cave where she and Nagar fast and sweat for days. When they emerge, their faces shine with the lustre of the spirit world.

'We go to the far north,' Hebera says. 'Across the frozen wastes to the mountains, where we will sleep.'

Malor spits his anger on the ground. 'You mean where we will die. Not even the meanest animal can eke out a living there.'

Nagar steps forward. 'We will not die.' She shows them all a finely polished orb of stone that glitters with a golden light. 'The spirits have given me this totem from the fire. It will lead us out of this world and into the one beyond, where our ancestors live.'

Malor huffs. 'And this is not death?'

Hebera takes Nagar's outstretched hand. 'The spirits say we will sleep, but we shall not die. Our clan will not prove to be the Last. Crow has shown me what is to come, and in the flames of the spirit fire I have seen our descendants thriving again in this world.'

*

So Ren-*ya* and her people leave their home and travel north to the foothills of the snowy mountains. There they light another great fire and chant through day and night. But Malor has been whispering to the people, questioning what Nagar says, and when Hebera asks who will be the first to go, no one steps forward.

Ren-*ya* is afraid too, but she knows her mother does not lie. 'I will go first,' she says.

Ren-*ya* lies down on the ice and the Last cover her with snow, leaving only her face open to the sky. Her mother puts the glittering stone under Ren-*ya*'s tongue. 'Sleep and have no fear,' she says. 'The ancestors will carry you safely to the spirit world.'

Nagar watches over her daughter until she sleeps. Then she takes the crystal orb from Ren-*ya*'s bloodless lips and covers her face with snow. Nagar lays the totem in the mouths of the Last and, one by one, they fall asleep.

Snow upon snow falls on their bodies and the Last are buried deep.

For a long time, there is nothing but snow and ice, nothing but the cold. Then, at last, a change comes.

The earth warms.

The glaciers begin to melt.

Part One

Poland, 1910

THE TASTE OF TREACHERY

Bela was woken by shouting – 'Up there! Look! Someone, help her!' – and, when she came to, she found herself standing high above the cobbled streets of Kraków, her toes curled over the edge of the steeply sloping roof.

For a moment, shock froze her to the spot. Far below, a crowd had gathered and, as Bela swayed over the yawning void, someone cried out, 'She's going to fall!'

Bela took a tiny step back from the edge, her heart hammering in her chest. In the houses on the other side of the street, people threw open their windows, hanging out as far as they dared to get a better view. Bela heard their terrified gasps as she dropped to a crouch on the tiles.

Don't look down, Bela told herself. But it was a humid summer night and half the city seemed to be out on the streets. She couldn't help catching glimpses of the people below, their upturned faces lit by the gas lamps: some horrified, others eager.

A voice came out of the darkness behind her. 'Oh my goodness! Bela! What are you doing out there?'

Bela slowly turned her head. The housekeeper and one of the maids were only a few feet away, leaning from the window of Bela's attic bedroom.

'Be careful!' They stretched their arms out, ready to grab her as, inch by inch, Bela crawled across the tiles towards them. A great cry of relief and disappointment rose up from the street as Bela climbed back through the window to safety.

'What on earth did you think you were doing?' the housekeeper said once she and the maid had got Bela back into bed. 'You could've been killed!'

Bela's body was still trembling. 'I . . . I was dreaming,' she managed to stammer out.

'About what?'

It was difficult to piece it all together. She remembered a black-and-white bird tapping at her window, and before that there had been someone standing at the bottom of her bed. A woman with auburn hair, just like Bela's.

'I was dreaming about my mother,' she said.

'Oh.' The housekeeper exchanged a knowing look with the maid and quickly changed the subject. 'Here.' She handed Bela a glass. 'Have something to drink.'

Bela gulped the water down, but it didn't wash away the cloying flavour of ashes that clung to her tongue. The woman in her dream had tasted of it.

'I dreamed my mother was dead.'

Three days later, Bela was summoned to the library where Great-aunt Olga was waiting for her. On the couch opposite was Olga's lawyer, Zabrowski. He sat motionless, his face and clothes so lacking in colour that he seemed more like an ageing sepia photograph than a living human being.

'Ah, Bela, there you are.' Olga got to her feet and smoothed the wrinkles from the fine silk of her skirt. 'Please sit down.'

Bela lowered herself cautiously into one of the plump velvet armchairs. She could tell from the sharp taste that hung in the air that something was wrong. Was she about to get another dressing-down for the sleepwalking incident? Olga had been furious, especially when she realized the whole street had witnessed Bela's 'shameful escapade'.

'I'm afraid I have some bad news.' Olga arranged

her face into what she clearly considered a sympathetic expression. 'I received a telegram today from your uncle in Siberia.'

Bela held her breath. Her mother lived in Uncle Viktor's house and there could only be one reason for him to send a telegram.

'I'm sorry to inform you,' Olga continued, 'that your mother has passed away.'

Since the dream, Bela had felt as if a great weight was hanging over her, and now Olga's cold words fell into her heart like stones. 'When?' she said.

'Three nights ago.'

Three nights? But that was when she woke up on the roof. She must have been dreaming of her mother at the very moment of her death. Bela remembered the silent figure who'd stood at the bottom of her bed. It had been more than a nightmare: it had been a visitation.

'Of course, it's very sad,' Aunt Olga continued. 'Although one can't help feeling that it may all be for the best.'

Bela couldn't believe what she was hearing. 'What do you mean, "for the best"?'

Olga's face took on a pained expression. 'I should have thought the benefits were obvious, in view of your mother's –' she raised a handkerchief to her mouth to smother the offending word – '*illness*.'

Bela's mouth flooded with the sick taste of shame. Her mother had suffered from a malady that was spoken of in whispers, behind closed doors, a condition that could not be mentioned in polite society. It was one thing to break a leg or catch the measles, quite another to be 'deranged'. The shame of it seeped out of the afflicted person and attached itself to their friends and relatives. Bela knew Olga was expecting her to end up the same way, to inherit the curse of madness from her mother.

Once Olga had dispensed a few more bland words of comfort, Bela was sent off to bed. But she had hardly made it up the first flight of stairs to her room before a syrupy taste escaped from a crack in the library door, floated up through the dusty air of the old house and reached Bela. She leaned over the banister and drew a long breath into her lungs. The flavour was one she'd often tasted on her aunt, but never as strongly as this. It seemed as sweet as sugar dust, but soon turned to bitterness on the back of her tongue. It was the taste of treachery.

Bela glided silently back down the stairs to the library and peered in. She could see Great-aunt Olga and Zabrowski, their heads together over a large mahogany desk.

'What are the terms?' Olga was saying.

Zabrowski replied in a voice as dry as his legal papers. 'Professor Novak has made a very generous offer. As his ward, she'll inherit Wilder House on his death.'

Olga huffed. 'What good is that to me?'

Zabrowski acknowledged his client's concern with a small bow. 'He promises to make a large cash payment for your trouble, but only if you send her to him in Siberia straight away.'

It was all Bela could do to remain hidden and quiet. How dare her aunt sell her off as if she was one of her possessions?

But Olga had no such misgivings. 'Well, that's settled then,' she said. 'After all, she can't stay here, especially after that incident on the roof. I dread to think how many people saw her.' Olga picked up a pen. 'Where should I sign?'

Zabrowski cleared his throat politely. 'There is just the matter of the girl's welfare to consider. Doesn't it

strike you as odd that Professor Novak is asking for the girl now? And why the urgency? He's shown no interest in her before, but now her mother's dead he immediately sends for her.'

Olga shrugged. 'As regards her welfare, I rather think I've done my bit. After all, I've fed and clothed the child since her father went off on his foolhardy expedition and disappeared.'

Zabrowski nodded. 'Indeed, madam. But the girl is what, thirteen? She'll be married off in a few years.'

Olga snorted. 'You men have no idea about these matters. Who would want to marry her?' She lowered her voice to a whisper. 'She won't be able to hide that hideous mark on her hand forever.'

Bela felt a stab of humiliation. The 'hideous mark' was a tattoo that Bela's mother had scratched into the palm of her hand when she was a baby. Olga said it was a disgrace and made Bela wear gloves to hide it.

Bela's great-aunt continued to list the reasons no one would ever want to marry her niece. 'The child is most disagreeable,' she said. 'And far too quick to give her opinion. Worse, she has no money, no property, nothing to make up for her . . . drawbacks.'

Zabrowski raised an eyebrow. 'You mean the mother?'

'Of course I mean the mother! Who else? The

woman was an *illiterate tribeswoman*. A lunatic. Who would want to marry into that? Especially now the girl is going the same way . . .' She sighed and in that exhaled breath, Bela caught the vinegary taste of her aunt's disapproval. 'It's for her own good. For the sake of the family's reputation, sacrifices must be made.' She leaned over the papers that lay on the desk and signed Bela away with a flourish.

Outside the library door, Bela closed her hands into fists. She had no choice about where she was sent, but of one thing she was certain: she would be nobody's sacrifice.